TRANSPARENT
blue.

K E N
K O E N I G

D1430443

Stewart Brooks Publishing, Inc.

Published by Stewart Brooks Publishing, Inc., Princeton, N.J., 1999

ISBN 1-928669-00-X

Library of Congress Catalog Card Number: 99-72567

Printed in the United States of America

Publisher's note:

This is a work of fiction. Names, characters, places, and incidents either are the product of the author's imagination or are used fictitiously, and any resemblance to actual persons, living or dead, or locales is entirely coincidental.

For information, please write to:

Stewart Brooks Publishing, Inc.
Marketing Department
66 Witherspoon Street, Suite 249
Princeton, NJ 08542

This book is dedicated to
three generations of the *Koenig family*.
My appreciation goes out to *my parents*,
who gave me the moral fiber and guidelines
for a solid family structure that became the
basis and underlying message of the book.

A heartfelt thanks also goes out to
my wife, Carolynn, who unselfishly
encouraged me to continue writing even
though it took my time away from her.
This was an especially giving position on
her part, considering that running my
advertising agency already takes up a
good ten to twelve hour day.
Carolynn is a never ending source of
inspiration for me. She never stops
believing in my ability to succeed,
"and therefore I am."

Lastly, I need to thank God
for *my children*. Without them,
I would not have fully understood
the impact of a parent's unparalleled
and unconditional love.

Embarkments 1

It was seemingly a journey to a new country. Full of new hopes, dreams and adventures. It was, however, a journey that would alter generations to follow.

The moist salt air lay frozen on Wilhelm's strong, handsome face as he stared out toward the dawning horizon of the cold, white-capped ocean. A million thoughts were swirling anxiously through his mind. Fear. Doubt. Excitement. And wonder. His thoughts shifted as wildly as the ocean lapping against the salt-coated hull of the ship deep below his feet. What would this new world be like? America. He had heard great stories of wealth and freedom. No matter what America was like, he was grateful to be escaping the war he would have been forced to enter in Germany in a few months when he reached 18. A war he didn't believe in. A bloody war he didn't have the commitment to fight. He knew deep in his soul that this lack of commitment came from a lack of loyalty toward Germany. It was 1914, and Germany had become a cruel and aggressive country, and he had a longing to live in America. He wondered how his parents would be, left in a homeland to survive a long, cold winter, and perhaps an even longer war. It was feared that the discovery of Wilhelm's treason would strip them of their wealth. Money his father had worked so very hard for. A large swell jerked the ship, and Wilhelm gripped the handrail tightly. A tear started to flow down his cheek but froze in place. He felt a great sense of guilt for leaving his parents to such a horrible future, when he was facing such a bright one. He remembered boyhood walks with his father, a distinguished gentleman who could be parentally tough when needed, but always had a soft heart especially when it came to Wilhelm. And a warm, calm feeling surrounded him as he thought of his mom, a beautiful woman, who would cuddle with him in front of a warm fire on cold winter days like this. Wilhelm slowly walked across the weathered wooden deck to look at the English port they had stopped at after his departure from France. A fog had rolled in and he could only see the blinking light of a lighthouse off in the distance. He felt lonely in the fog. And as he stared out at the blinking light, slipping slowly into oblivion, he had a strange eerie sense of doom and remorse. "This would begin the longest part of the journey," he thought.

Suddenly a firm grip wrapped around Wilhelm's arm. "Wilhelm Strauss?" asked the ship steward.

"I am sorry. You startled me. Yes, I am Wilhelm," he replied.

The steward, a ruddy Englishman with a reddish handlebar mustache and a pale face ravaged by smallpox demanded, "You are wanted in the captain's quarters."

"Yes, certainly," replied Wilhelm with an air of confidence. Wilhelm was frightened by the steward's tone. Deep within Wilhelm's confident outward appearance was a horrible fear that he had been discovered by the German army for fleeing the country before enlistment. He followed the steward toward the captain's quarters. The portly, balding captain, also an Englishman, stood at the ship's controls.

"Wilhelm Strauss?" asked the captain. He looked up into Wilhelm's piercing steel blue eyes and chiseled face, tanned by the sun and wind from standing out on the ship's deck.

"Yes sir," he replied, nervously brushing his thick black hair back with his callused hands.

"We have an urgent message for you. You may read it in the guest quarters," he said pointing to a room just off the main helm. His voice cracked slightly as he guided Wilhelm to the door of the comfortable room filled with oak and red leather. There was a strong musty feel to the room, with an odor of wood weathered by the sea. Wilhelm's hands began to quiver as he anxiously made his way toward the worn, cold couch.

He read: "Mother has died... Consumption... Do not come back... You cannot contact me... Do not fear for me... Live a good life... My love to you forever my son... Dad."

Wilhelm looked up at first in disbelief. The captain, who was watching Wilhelm read the message, quickly shut the door to the guest quarters. Left alone, Wilhelm's hands began to tremble uncontrollably. Then his entire body began to lurch in agony. He couldn't breathe, and sat gasping for air. Until suddenly, a violent, wrenching cry of pain came out of the depths of his insides. The steward came in sheepishly, looking down at the floor, with a glass of Scotch, and helped Wilhelm's trembling hand guide the glass to his parched, chapped lips. "Thank you sir. Now please leave me be," Wilhelm struggled to get the words out with dignity. He sat silently listening to each wooden floorboard creak as the steward quietly stepped toward the door. He could hear only the sounds of seagulls and the rough ocean outside. Wilhelm instinctively stood, but his legs buckled. He sat back down, and began to sob louder and harder. The only reason he would have stayed in Germany was for his intense love of his parents. Parents so giving and loving, he felt a great sense of guilt in leaving them. Yet all of the arrangements for Wilhelm to leave the country were made by them. And his father, a wealthy jeweler, had made sure he had money in his pocket to start the journey. His mother, with her flowing black hair, and entrancing blue eyes like his own, who was well received in all of the most lofty of social settings, was the one who felt strongest about his leaving.

"You must leave," she would say, hiding the pain she would feel in missing her son through a flash of her smile which showed a dimple on one cheek. "We will follow you. I promise," she would say, while wiping the tears from her eyes. Maybe this was true, Wilhelm thought. Maybe this is the only way she was able to follow me. To watch over me. This thought began to make him feel better, and his hands stopped trembling somewhat. He used the sleeves of his long, heavy overcoat to wipe away his tears. His eyes were still swollen, but he was beginning to focus again. The ship steward opened the squeaking door and put only his head through the opening. Seeing that Wilhelm was no longer hysterical, he slowly and humbly walked over toward him. Each step letting out a prolonged squeal of the floorboards.

"May I see you back to your cabin, sir?" he asked in a quiet stutter.

"I thank you, but I can make it on my own," Wilhelm replied graciously.

Downing the remaining Scotch, Wilhelm slowly got up, still holding on to the arm of the couch for support. Without looking up, he made his way silently across the room, through the doorway into the main cabin. The captain instantly appeared almost obtrusively in his face. "Are you OK now, Heir Strauss?"

"Yes, thank you," Wilhelm whispered, his voice too hoarse to speak. Without further conversation or eye contact, Wilhelm exited the helm, looking only at his feet to make certain he didn't stumble. He couldn't bear the thought of the sunlight that had burned through the fog as they ventured further out to sea. The glaring brilliance of the sun and the reflection on the pristine water were too much in contrast for this solemn occasion. He also kept his gaze downward, because as he began to make his way down the deck, he could see that a great many passengers were about to see the onset of what would be a glorious day. The first sunny day since they had left France.

He could feel that the temperature had gone up well above what it had been, and he unbuttoned his heavy coat as he walked. Beginning to feel self-conscious about his swelled eyes, he began to walk more and more rapidly hoping to reach his room without too much notice. This was not an easy task for such a large, handsome man. But he concentrated on putting one foot in front of the other without losing balance.

As he turned the corner of his cabin hallway, he bumped into someone. At first, he was going to keep walking without a word, but instead he made eye contact. "Excuse me," he said gruffly. It was a woman, he would guess about 20, dressed in a floor length green overcoat, that shimmered in the sunlight, with a rather large hat of the same color and very large, emerald-colored eyes to match.

"Are you all right?" she asked inquisitively, as she gazed into Wilhelm's swollen red eyes.

"Yes," said Wilhelm quickly, as he turned to continue his pace down the hall.

"No, no. Not because of that, because you look as if you're not all right." Her heavy French accent was now absolutely apparent. Wilhelm kept walking without a reply. "Arrogant," she whispered under her breath. "How rude." Yet as she made her way onto the deck, she couldn't help thinking of the troubled look in the young man's beautiful blue eyes. Eyes so crystal blue, they almost seemed transparent. As if she could see through them, right down to the innocence of his very soul.

For the next several days and nights, Wilhelm stayed in his cabin. He ordered in what little food he could eat. He did so only to keep his strength, as an appetite eluded him. Every once in a while he would take a walk out on the deck, or simply stand at the handrail staring blindly into the churning sea. Many times these walks took place in the middle of the night, when he knew that nobody would interrupt his solitude. He was beginning to long for the end of the journey, and for a fresh start in the new land. He had been taught and trained as a jewelry engraver by his father and with a thousand dollars sewed into the lining of his suitcase, he knew he didn't have to worry about money from the onset. In fact, this was enough money to last him for a year of comfortable living. Thinking of his new life was all he could concentrate on now, as it was medicine for the emptiness he was feeling deep inside. According to his calendar, he should be there in the next two days.

A sudden knock on the door startled him out of a daze. He looked out of his porthole, disoriented. It was daylight. About midday, from the looks of the sun. He hurriedly grabbed a robe from the foot of his bed and made his way to the door. "Just a minute," he yelled. He opened the door to find a smiling, polite ship steward.

"For you, Heir Strauss," the steward said as he handed him an important looking envelope sealed with a gold emblem. Wilhelm shut the door without a reply. His heart seemed to pause and then race, as the last message he was handed aboard this ship had sent his entire world into a tailspin. His hands shook as he read the envelope. However, from the looks of this envelope, it was clear this was of a friend-lier nature. An invitation, perhaps. He opened it.

"The Captain requests your company at his table for dinner this evening, 6:00 sharp."

"Oh, I couldn't," he thought to himself. He sat down on the edge of his bed. His eyes darted from the invitation to the sky outside the porthole and back to his pillow which still lay in quiet seclusive darkness. It seemed like hours that he sat, contemplating.

Then with a surge of conviction, he stood up strongly and said out loud, "It's time. It's time to get on with my life. I will go." His decision was none to soon, as he looked at the shelf clock and realized it was already 5:30. "Oh my goodness, I've got to shave."

He walked over to the tiny mirror on the wall

and was shocked by his own unkempt image. He had obviously lost weight. Some 10 or even 15 pounds, he thought. And a shave was well in order. It felt good to get back into life. He took his tuxedo out of the closet, and made his way down the hall to take a warm bath. After bathing, Wilhelm felt somewhat renewed, and was starting to feel human again. While dressing, he glanced in the mirror to comb his hair and thought, "Not a bad looking gentleman. Maybe a pound or two underweight. But not a bad looking gentleman, I am."

It was 5:50, so he quickly rounded the hallway up to the main ballroom. As he entered, the first thing that struck him was the enormity of the room. And how brilliantly sparkling the massive crystal chandeliers were, all lit up with a multitude of lights. "Breathtaking." The carpeting was a crimson color, and all of the fixtures were gold, or at least gold plated he thought. The table and chairs, which were richly upholstered with a satin-like gold cloth, were made of good solid mahogany. And everyone looked so lively and sophisticated. "It's a shame I've stayed in my room. I've missed all this," he thought. "Perhaps it just looks so impressive because I've been in my room so long," he chuckled to himself. "Can I direct you, sir?" an attendant asked.

"Oh, yes, please. I'm looking for the captain's table."

"Right this way, sir." He followed the attendant to a long table located at the front of the dining room. The table was decorated with white lilies, which were so large, he could barely make out the other passengers who were already seated.

Upon approaching the table, the captain, actually a rather obnoxious man, however well-meaning, jumped up from his seat, as if Wilhelm were a celebrity. All of the passengers at the surrounding tables craned their necks to see who was being greeted so heartily.

"How are you Heir Strauss?" asked the captain in a concerned yet positive tone.

"Just fine, thank you. And thank you for your concern," said Wilhelm. He was surprised that his voice cracked while replying. "I'm certainly not over my emotions," he thought to himself.

The captain ushered him to the seat next to his own.

"Ladies and gentlemen, let me introduce you to Wilhelm Strauss."

"Strauss is an elite name in Germany. Are you related to the Strauss family in Hanover Province?" asked a rather piggish looking American woman in a bright blue evening gown.

"No. No relation that I know of."

The woman giggled and lifted her napkin to cover her mouth. Her husband, a mousy, milk toasty looking man, looked embarrassed. Wilhelm couldn't stop looking at the monstrous blue feather that was sticking out of her hair. It seemed as if she had been attacked by a prehistoric bird of some sort. And as the waiter came by to fill her water glass, it stuck in his face and made him sneeze.

Wilhelm began to gaze around the table. Next to this woman's husband was the most attractive woman he had ever seen. Dark hair, softly glowing white skin, and crystal clear green eyes. "Not the usual green eyes that you see on the everyday person," he thought. These were green eyes the color of which he had only seen before in the finest emeralds in his father's jewelry store. She was wearing a white satin evening gown. And her hair was pulled tightly back so that you could distinctly see her face. "Her features look as though they are made of fine porcelain," he thought. So fine. So perfect. Yet, so mysterious, and different. He realized he was staring, and although the lady with the feather was still talking to him, asking him if he was a German dignitary or something, he was transfixed on a woman who was most obviously ignoring him.

The lady with the blue feather asked Wilhelm if he knew Maria, as she motioned to the mysterious woman in white. At that point Maria looked up at Wilhelm with a gaze as cold as ice and snapped, "We've met." Then she nervously looked back down at her salad.

"I beg your pardon miss, but I don't believe we have," insisted Wilhelm, confused by her disdain.

"You bumped into me the other day. In fact, I thought you were just a rude American," Maria blurted in anger. The woman with the feather looked obviously offended. Wilhelm stared at her in silence. He was perplexed.

"When did we meet, Maria? I really don't recall. And I think I would recall someone as lovely as you."

Maria looked up at him and began to melt. "The other day... we bumped into each other."

Suddenly Wilhelm remembered the beautiful French woman in the green dress. "Oh, of course. I am sorry. I wasn't feeling myself," Wilhelm said, clearing his throat as he spoke.

At that point the captain leaned over to Maria, and whispered something in her ear. She turned crimson, and then paled. Her eyes seemed to well up. She looked sheepishly at Wilhelm.

"You would perhaps like to go for a stroll after dinner?" she said, her broken English beginning to show.

"I think I would like that," responded Wilhelm with a warm smile.

After a long, but pleasant dinner, Wilhelm arose from his chair and offered his arm to Maria. She responded.

"Perhaps we should gather our coats before we go outside," suggested Maria.

"Yes, I guess you're right," laughed Wilhelm.

"Why don't we meet at the same spot that we originally bumped into each other?" Maria suggested.

Wilhelm agreed, and quietly kissed Maria's hand.

As he walked to his room he had a feeling of excitement and relief. Relief that something in his life was finally going right. His first night out since his tragedy, and he was going for a romantic evening stroll with the most beautiful woman on the ship. Life was beginning to take an upturn.

Maria placed the key in her door and noticed that it was not locked. "I could have sworn I locked this before leaving," she thought to herself. She entered the darkened room and felt her way along the wall to find the desk light. The moon let in some light through the porthole and her eyes were beginning to adjust. It was then she thought she saw something in the corner of the room. It looked like the silhouette of a person. She stood frozen in fear. Between the lapping of the waves hitting the hard, steel exterior of the ship, she could hear something else. Breathing. Faint breathing. Terrified, she screamed and turned to make her way to the door. As she fled in the darkness, her foot got caught on the bottom of the bed, and she could hear and sense that an unwelcome visitor was scurrying toward her. Frantically she reached for the door handle. She had made it, and opened the door to reveal a hopeful beam of light emitting from the hallway. But the door was slammed shut, and the strong intruder pushed her onto the bed. Maria was desperately trying to catch her breath, but began to hyperventilate between small screeches and sobs. She couldn't scream. Try as she might, she was prevented by her own horror. Suddenly the lamp was lit, and flickering in the darkness was a clearer image. Standing over her was a dark, tall and very large man with a stubbed nose that had been broken more than once and a face ravaged with deep, ugly scars.

"You fool!" Maria shouted in an angry whisper. "You know you're not supposed to come here. You nearly scared me to death."

"I had to come," responded the man. "I had to know. Did you meet him? Did it work?"

"Yes, it worked. He doesn't suspect a thing," Maria said, her green eyes twisted into an evil snarl.

"What does he look like?" asked the man.

"He's quite handsome, in a Nordic sort of way," responded Maria.

The man slapped her violently. "I mean, what is he wearing? What color hair does he have?" asked the man angrily.

"See for yourself. We are going for a stroll on the deck. I will walk him by the porthole," she said in a coy and teasing tone. Quickly,

Maria got up, whisked her coat from the closet and walked out of the room, slamming the door behind her. The dark man smirked, and walked over to position himself for a view out the porthole.

Maria calmed her nerves as she walked down the long white hallway. She maneuvered herself like a cat stalking her prey. Dressed in a floor length white mink, her green eyes shimmered as she walked by each wall lamp. She hoped Wilhelm would be waiting at the end of the hallway, watching her dramatic approach as she knew this theatrical entrance would help to web her victim. She grew angry as she approached their meeting spot without a sign of him. This was not at all the way she imagined it. As she neared the end of the hallway, she was startled by someone quickly turning the corner. She clutched her heart. It was Wilhelm. He was reenacting the scene from days earlier when he was so rude. This time he smiled. "Enchanté," Wilhelm said in a warm seductive voice.

"Not at all," Maria replied in her French accent.

Wilhelm stopped for a split second and thought, "That was a strange reply for a Frenchie."

But the thought quickly fleeted. Instead he was stunned by the vision he saw before him, and he politely offered his arm. It seemed that they walked all night, strolling the deck and exploring different areas of the ship. Maria spoke of her family life in Paris, her schooling, and of the modeling career she was embarking on in New York. Wilhelm was not at all surprised to hear that she was born of royalty, and that her father was a very successful clothier. Wilhelm spoke of his family too. He told her of the death of his mother, and tearfully confided that he was experiencing loneliness like he had never known before. He told her of his father and the war he was escaping. He told her about the money his father gave him to start a new life. Maria held him tightly when he spoke. She told him she would watch over him, and never leave him, and they would go to New York together.

"I feel as though I've had the worst time of my life, and the best time of my life, in a matter of days," Wilhelm said with emotional laughter.

"I know we haven't known each other very long, but I feel very fond of you," Maria replied.

The wind was blowing furiously out on the deck as they stood holding hands, talking. Wilhelm noticed how Maria's fine features looked even more beautiful accentuated by the moonlight.

"I'm cold", she said, looking up into his power-ful eyes. He hugged her tightly, and they kissed. Suddenly, Maria stopped and turned her head. "It's late, and I really should get back to my cabin."

Wilhelm obliged, and escorted her to her room. Not a word was spoken, and both Wilhelm and Maria were deep in thought. It was as if neither wanted to speak for chance something might be said that might interfere with this magical evening. Wilhelm's heart raced. He felt he was in love. Although he had dated girls in Germany, this was different. Very different. Maria searched for her key buried deep in her pocket, and asked quietly, "Will I see you tomorrow?"

"Breakfast, at 8:00," replied Wilhelm, relieved she asked.

"Ten o'clock, and it's a date. I need my beauty sleep," she said coyly.

Wilhelm laughed. "Ten o'clock it is. And no, you don't need beauty sleep at all."

Maria made her way into the cabin, looking into Wilhelm's eyes lovingly, until the door shut.

"Well, did you see him?" she asked her dark companion.

"Yeah, I saw him. Big German guy. Does he have money, or what?"

"Oh, he's got money. In fact Heir Daddy gave him a load of money that he's got right here on the ship," she said gleefully.

"Where is it?"

"Give me some time. I'll find out," she replied with arrogance. "And what does enchanté mean anyway?"

"It means nice to meet you Maria. You should know that!"

"Can I get some sleep now?" she asked, ignoring his anger. The companion opened the door slowly, stuck his head out, and then left without making a sound. Maria went to bed.

Maria and Wilhelm spent the next day together, laughing, dining, and dancing. "I can't remember being happier," Wilhelm blurted as they took a stroll after dinner. "I want you to have this," Wilhelm said as he pulled a simple silver ring out of his pocket.

"No, I couldn't..." Maria replied.

"I want you to. It was my mother's. She said to give it to the girl of my dreams. I know she's smiling down on this right now. Don't worry, it's not valuable in dollars. Its value is in sentiment," Wilhelm said smiling.

Maria nodded and put the ring on, and her eyes welled with tears as she looked up into Wilhelm's transparent blue eyes.

"Tomorrow we will be in New York. Where will you be? How will I reach you?" asked Wilhelm anxiously.

"Here, let me write you my address. I'll be staying with my uncle on West Park," Maria confided as she drew a pen from the desk in the ship lobby, and wrote down her address.

"Park Avenue. I've heard of Park Avenue. It must be very beautiful," Wilhelm said.

"Where will you stay? How will you pay for a place to stay when you don't have a job yet?" Maria asked with concern.

"You've forgotten. My father gave me money to make this journey and establish my new life in America," Wilhelm replied proudly.

"Isn't that dangerous? Where do you hide such a great amount of money?" Maria asked with a concerned expression.

"It is sewn into the lining of my luggage trunk," Wilhelm proudly whispered, feeling very clever about how well he had hidden his fortune.

The following morning, Wilhelm awoke to sunshine streaming through his porthole. It felt warm on his face. And as he realized this was the day he had been waiting for, his heart began to race with anticipation. He was startled by a knock on the door. It was Maria, inviting him to breakfast. "I'll be there in 30 minutes," Wilhelm told her. He bounded down the hall to take a bath and shave, and then joined Maria in the restaurant. As they sat eating, there was a crowd gathering along the deck guardrail.

He heard someone say in hushed excitement, "America!"

Quickly grabbing Maria's hand, he rushed her outside to join the others. Wilhelm gasped with emotion as he caught a glimpse of the Statue of Liberty far off in the hazy distance.

"Isn't that the most beautiful sight you have ever seen?" he asked.

Maria looked up at him. "No, it's not," she said with a smirk, gazing up into his sparkling blue eyes.

Wilhelm didn't hear her, for now the ship was roaring with the cries of cheers and hollers of the excited passengers.

"I guess we should go below and get ready to debark," Maria said anxiously.

Wilhelm agreed and they went to their cabins.

When they arrived at the harbor, there was a frenzy of passengers waiting to get off the ship only to wait on long lines for processing. Wilhelm, wheeling his trunk behind him, quickly ran down the long hallway to Maria's cabin. Her door was open so he went in. To his astonishment, she wasn't there. Although they hadn't discussed it, he was sure she would be waiting for him. He immediately ran out to the deck, where hundreds of passengers were bustling and making their way, luggage in hand, down the gangplank. He strained to look for Maria, but she was nowhere to be found. If he didn't move down the gangplank now, surely he would be trampled. Still no Maria. He grew more and more anxious.

"Thank goodness I have her address. If I never find her again in this crowd, at least I'll find her at home," he thought.

As he made his way down the long white gangplank, he held the railing with one hand and glanced back up to the ship, still searching for Maria.

"I must remember, if I am asked, that I am here only for a week to meet with jewelers on behalf of my father's business," he thought.

He had heard stories of how horribly the American government treated illegal immigrants. His father had prepared him well for his arrival, and had carefully planned for all of the documentation and fees ahead of his departure from home. In fact, his departure from the ship all seemed a blur of activity and confusion. He knew now that he was headed for American soil, to stay. He realized he would need some money, so once he put his feet on the dock, he retreated to a deserted area of the shipyard where he would be alone. Digging deep into his long, warm overcoat, he pulled out the key to his trunk. He quickly glanced around the dock to make sure nobody was watching him, and positioned the key in his hand to slit open the sewn lining. A heavy, sick feeling landed deep in his gut as he looked at the lining. It had already been slit. He pushed the large brown trunk open onto the pavement and furiously pushed his clothes aside, unable to believe what he was seeing. He felt for the money, and then pushed his hand into the lining, groping for anything! It was gone! All of it! His eyes darted back and forth across the dock area. He was in shock, and all other sounds were cut off. He pushed his hand into the lining again. Deeper and deeper. He shifted his clothes to the other side of the trunk.

"Maybe I made a mistake," he thought. "Maybe it was this side of the trunk."

He took his key and ripped open the lining. "Nothing," he thought, falling down to his knees. He cupped his hands around his eyes. "Calm down. Don't panic. Let me look again. I'm sure this is a mistake. It must be here." When he lowered his hands, his eyes fixed on the lining again. "It's no use. It's gone," he thought. He sat motionless for hours, staring at the slit lining. "I will deal with this. I will get by. I will survive," he thought. "What choice do I have?" He didn't know whether he was angry or scared. In fact, he now felt emotionless.

Suddenly he realized he was going to be sick, and turned his head away from his belongings.

His entire body seemed to convulse with each spasm. Afterward he slowly rose to his feet, closed up the trunk and made his way toward the building that lay in front of the dock. An instinct to survive had taken over. The city ahead of him looked dark and dirty. Busy, with more people he had ever seen assembled in one place, all hurrying and moving quickly. Most of the other passengers had family waiting for them. There were tearful reunions and a muffled roar of joyous cheers all around him. He felt empty again. Alone. More alone than he ever felt before.

"Where is Maria?" he asked out loud to himself. "She will help me." "Maria," he thought. A horrible thought entered his mind. "Maria is the only person who knew about the money. But she wouldn't do this to me," he thought.

A thousand questions circled in his mind. But he didn't have time to pursue any of them. "I need to find a place to stay. A way to eat. With no money," he thought, beginning to panic again. "The answer is to find Maria," he said to himself as he pulled her address from his pocket. "She will help me. She will give me a place to stay. Perhaps I should talk to a police-man," he thought as he began to walk down the busy street. He had spotted a friendly look-ing policeman who pushed his hat up with his billy club as he passed, as if to offer a polite hello to the foreigner without speaking. Wilhelm's mother had taught him English as a second language and it was spoken quite fluently around the house with little or no trace of an accent. "I can't. Too risky. Too many questions," he thought as he turned around several times, sizing up the officer. He kept walking.

A horse drawn carriage was pulling up behind him as he turned another corner. "The next friendly looking person I see, I will ask where Park Avenue is," he thought to himself.

"Whoa!" calmed a coachman, yelling out amidst all the bustle of the city. As Wilhelm turned to look, he recognized the lady with the feather, and her husband. She smiled and asked Wilhelm if he would like a ride.

His face lit up "Yes. Yes. I would. Thank you." Wilhelm was so relieved to see a familiar face in this monstrous city of strangers. She looked friendlier now, not so piggish, just round. She wore a plain black hat that wrapped around her face to keep her warm, and her cheeks were pink from the cold wind that came whipping around the shadows of the tall buildings lining the streets.

"Where are you staying?" she asked.

"I don't know," Wilhelm responded. "But I have a friend on Park Avenue."

"Maria?" asked the woman, in an obviously disapproving, motherly tone. Wilhelm nodded, and there was an uneasy silence set against the clip-clop of the horse.

"I've been robbed," Wilhelm blurted.

"Oh my goodness!" screeched the woman.

"You've got to notify the police," her husband demanded.

Wilhelm was uncomfortable with the direction the conversation was headed, and wished he hadn't mentioned the robbery. "This woman is just the type that won't relent. She'll surely contact the police," he thought.

"I'm very sorry, but I've forgotten your names," he said embarrassed.

The woman politely smiled and said with a biting tone, "I am Heidi Brunning and this is my husband, Frederick Brunning."

"You are of German decent!" Wilhelm acknowledged gleefully.

"Why did you think we instantly took a liking to you?" she chuckled.

"It's late, and you're tired. You will stay with us tonight," she said in a demanding yet motherly tone.

At first Wilhelm could think of nothing but Maria. He thought, "If I stay with them tonight, it will slow me down from finding her. But then again, if I don't find her, I will be penniless in a big city. All alone."

"Thank you. You're very kind," Wilhelm responded.

As they traveled up the street, Wilhelm noticed that there seemed to be different pockets of communities. Further into the heart of the city, the homes that lined the streets were becoming beautiful. Made of a brown stone that he hadn't seen before. And they were huddled right next to each other as if they were ready to face the ominous city together as a team. Not at all the way he pictured America. He thought this would be a country full of open land, not a cramped city. The people on the streets were dressed in the finest clothing he had ever seen. And there seemed to be everything – shops, restaurants, museums, theaters, everywhere. He found it simultaneously exhilarating and intimidating.

"I think I will like it here. It seems very exciting," Wilhelm thought, as he sat motionless, speechless, absorbing the sights as they traveled.

The carriage pulled over in front of one of the brownstone buildings, and the Brunnings' belongings were deposited on the large brick sidewalk. The driver held Mrs. Brunning's hand. She needed the help. And Wilhelm carried her bag as well as his own up the stairs to the front door. Mrs. Brunning used the elaborate door knocker. Shaped like a lion's head, the solid brass construction made a loud clanging noise as it hit the large white door. Wilhelm stood in awe as a young woman opened the door. She was athletic looking, with large, clear blue eyes and white blond hair that was pulled back by a blue ribbon. Her hair cascaded down behind her shoulders in loose curls. She was clearly of German decent, with strong, classic features. There was no mistaking it. Not entirely feminine though. There was a sharp strength to her face. But classic and pretty. She was obviously confused when she opened the door, since there was a stranger with her parents.

Battered and Bruised 2

A horrific throbbing sensation jolted through Maria's brow as she opened her eyes to squint, allowing only some sunlight to penetrate her sight. She looked around the room, frightened and frantic, trying to orient herself to her surroundings. The room was dark, except for the beam of light squeezing in through the bottom of the drawn curtains, radiating into her eyes. The walls of the room were dirty and worn. The heavy cloth curtains were a dark green, which matched the peeling, thickly painted trim of the room. She began to stretch and yawn as she realized she was back home in New York. She looked toward the light streaming in from the window, and a cloud of dust swirled in the air. The room carried a dank, musty odor. She covered her eye in pain, and remembered that she had been punched, and then must have been knocked unconscious. Her soft, fragile hand slowly moved from her swollen eye down to her neck, then down her chest, and torso. She was still dressed as she was when she hurriedly left the ship.

"I'm covered with blood," she realized as her hand made an exhausting journey down the length of her body. Her head pulsed with pain and she closed her eyes and slumped back down on the floor. Minutes passed before she opened her eyes again to look around the room. She began to laugh, at first quietly, and then more hysterically. Her laughter became loud sobs, as the tears rolled down her bruised and swollen face.

"What irony," she thought. "I'm right back where I started from. Except now, I have physical pain to go along with my anguish. It all had seemed like such a good plan," she thought. "A way out of this horrible life."

Maria slowly got up from the floor where she had been sleeping and sat up on the edge of her bed, her head still throbbing with every slow, deliberate movement. She began contemplating the devastating events that had taken place over the last couple of months. "How did it start?" she thought as she carefully peeled off her bloodied clothing. "It all started the day I met Robert." Robert, the dark stranger that accompanied her on her trip, had met her on the street one day as she walked home from her job in the shoe factory. She remembered her first impression as he approached her. "I'm going to be robbed," she had feared. But instead, he smiled, tipped his hat, and asked her if she would like to be a fashion model. An unlikely offering coming from this ghoulish man, she had thought. But she stopped to talk. Somewhat out of intrigue. Somewhat out of fear. That evening Robert took her to dinner. Maria recalled that he didn't look so ugly as she got to know him. In fact, he was so charming that she was amazed that his previously hideous features had grown into character. He was rugged looking. Manly looking. Not scary, at all.

Robert explained over dinner that he had connections in both New York and Paris, and with Maria's extraordinary looks, he could most certainly make her into the toast of the fashion industry. "He has tapped into my very personal dreams," Maria had thought. "Paris." The very mention had sent her into a spiral of fantasy. "I was hooked, instantly," Maria thought as she pounded her bed in anger, fighting back the tears.

Robert had arranged everything. They would arrive in Paris in style. Maria would be lavished in expensive evening gowns, jewels and minks. They would make the rounds of all of his high profile contacts, and would stay in Paris until she was a celebrity. The very next day, Robert took her to the finest clothiers on Park Avenue, and then to Chalfont's where she picked out a ruby and diamond necklace that draped down the middle of her neck, as well as a diamond tiara. It was like some magnificent fantasy. A whirlwind. She felt like a princess. He even helped her with her hair and makeup. He made her cut back on the heavy makeup she used to apply.

"Not so much rouge," he would demand.

And it was Robert's suggestion that she wear her hair up, always pulled starkly away from her face. Maria was amazed. She would sit for hours after Robert dropped her off at her apartment, just gazing at herself in the mirror.

"I really do appear regal," she thought.

Robert would spend the next week with her, correcting her New York dialect, and redoing her look to perfection. The one thing he didn't have to correct was her walk. Maria had a naturally elegant manner, and she walked with an air of sophistication. Even when she had been dressed in old, torn clothing, she carried herself like royalty.

Finally the big day had arrived, and Maria felt like a child at Christmas. She sat on the corner of her bed, anxiously waiting for Robert's carriage to pull up outside. She had been dressed for hours, and she looked beautiful, decorated in a burgundy dress with a matching hat that swirled from the peak of her forehead to the nape of her neck. Her perfect, milky face shimmered with purity. When Robert's carriage arrived, Maria grabbed her luggage and rapidly exited her apartment. "I hope I never see you again," she smirked, looking around the old depressing room. As she walked down the hallway, her neighbors, who saw her every day without taking much notice, stopped dead in their tracks, mouths open, as if they were in shock. Robert met her at the stairwell and helped her with her luggage. "He was a true gentleman and my own personal dream maker," she had thought.

As they traveled to the ship, crowds of people would turn around to stare. Not only at Maria, but at Robert. They were such an unusual pairing. An ugly, dark man with a broken face, and a silky, refined woman in the finest of clothing. He also insisted that they not be seen together on the ship, as it would seem improper to the other passengers that a single man and woman would be traveling together without escorts. And although they separated just before boarding the ship, Robert remained her teacher. They secretly met every morning in Maria's room. He would teach and drill her on proper diction. He taught her French.

"You'll need to know some French to get by in Paris," he would constantly remind her.

"He seemed to always be thinking of me," Maria recalled. She remembered that on several occasions, Robert began to scare her. He would become enraged when she wasn't learning quickly enough. And he would punch his large fist into a wall, or throw something across the room. Maria would sit paralyzed in fear, silent, until his rage passed. As the ship neared the French port, Robert entered her room for their usual morning meeting. Maria remembered his face that one particular morning. It was more serious than usual and she was afraid of what might be coming. "With good reason," she thought. Robert explained that they wouldn't be debarking in France. They would be staying on the ship and returning immediately. It was then Maria learned of his true motives. He stood as he explained, and paced the floor nervously. Maria sat quietly, scared, as she watched this dark, towering man unravel his true self in front of her. He seemed like a horrible monster now. Not at all likable or handsome in any way. Just ugly and evil.

The plan was to use Maria as a lure for a man with money. She would find a way to gain his trust, and then Robert would find a way to get the money. He would share it with her. She was to use a French accent so that it would help to throw off any chances of discovering their identities should anything go wrong.

"And if I don't go along with this plot of yours?" Maria stared into his eyes with venomous anger.

"Then I will twist your head until your neck breaks," Robert replied, staring back into her eyes with a cold dark glare that sent a chill of fear down Maria's spine. Maria hadn't expected this response. And she remembered feeling as if she just wanted to run away from him. But there was nowhere to go. She was trapped at sea, and this large ship they were on seemed so tiny, so claustrophobic now. When Robert finished his explanation, Maria just sat motionless, staring directly into his eyes. She had never felt such passionate hatred. Robert glared back at her with absolutely no emotion in his eyes. It made her skin crawl.

"Not only is this man evil, but he has no human emotion at all," she thought. Robert finally turned and left the room. Maria sat down on the edge of the hard wooden chair in the corner of her cabin. She dug her nails into the thick satin dress she was wearing and twisted it, and twisted it, until her hands were tired. "I'll do it," she thought regretfully. "What else can I do? I'll do it. I'll get money for it. And I won't put myself in danger. I know it's wrong and I hate him for making me. But I'll do it. And I'll do it well. But he's going to split it with me, or I'll go to the police," she plotted angrily. She bolted up off the edge of the chair and looked at her face in the mirror. Using her sleeve, she angrily wiped away her tears, and blinked her eyes long and hard to make them stop.

Maria went through the next several days as if she were doing time in a prison. She had resigned herself to her fate. Robert had left her alone during this period, except for one brief visit when he poked his head into her cabin to make sure she was okay. Maria remembered that he seemed sheepish on this occasion, and she reacted without emotion, telling him she was fine. It seemed like an eternity to Maria, but finally she heard the sounds of life outside her cabin, and the ship whistle blew loudly to announce their departure. She peered out of her small porthole and watched the land sink into a vast watery oblivion. Now Robert began visiting her cabin every morning again, with the usual lessons in the social graces. He would stare at her every night in the dining room, and the following mornings he would critique her behavior.

"You grabbed the wrong fork. A real lady wouldn't be so loud. You should dab your mouth gracefully with your napkin," he would scold.

Maria would sit each morning enduring each lecture. Then one afternoon she bumped into a stranger. Wilhelm. And the next morning she proudly reported to Robert she had met his mark. She explained as best she could what he looked like, and then arranged for Robert to see them the night they went for their first stroll. She reported everything to Robert. Where he was from. Who his parents were.

The death of his mother. The money! And where it was hidden! She was confused by Robert's behavior whenever she described him as handsome. He was clearly angered by such talk. But she assumed it was out of fear that if she began to care for Wilhelm, she may not carry out their mission.

Finally the morning came when Maria was to join Wilhelm for breakfast. She remembered getting up early that morning. She took a long, deliberate walk on the deck. It was cold out, and the steam from the ship's engines seemed to encircle the entire ship with white billowing hope. The water was white capped. But the sun rising slowly was the most beautiful and peaceful scene she had ever seen. The ship was quiet, as barely anyone else was about at that hour. And she recalled the sound of seagulls. As she turned the corner of the deck, the warm, orange sun felt so good on her face. She stopped to inhale the breathtaking horizon. And then suddenly, she remembered what she had to do. Her jaw dropped. Her shoulders settled. And she began to walk slowly again. She kept reminding herself that she had decided to do this. And surely she would be beaten if she didn't.

Now Maria began to walk faster, as if not to think. Instead, concentrating on getting the job done and over with. "Good morning, Mademoiselle," said the ship steward as she passed him walking down the narrow hallway. When she arrived at Wilhelm's door, she went to knock, then retracted her hand, pausing to collect her thoughts. Then she proceeded. After inviting him to breakfast she went back up to the dining room to wait for him. The deck was beginning to rapidly fill with people, all bustling about in anticipation of seeing land. Maria had seen this land before, and couldn't care less. Shortly after breakfast with Wilhelm, the crowd began carrying on about seeing the Statue of Liberty. All she could think was that Robert had by now made his way into Wilhelm's room and had taken all of his money. She couldn't look him in the eyes. And so she suggested that they go to their rooms and pack.

As she was packing, she suddenly froze in place. Something had been gnawing away at her for days, but she couldn't quite grasp what it was.

"Oh my God. I'm in love with him." She was shocked at her revelation. Maria's hands began to shake. "I won't let Robert get away with it," she shrieked. She pushed her door open and ran up the long hallway, up the white wooden stairs with her long white mink coat blowing in the wind behind her. She tripped as she ran, and her shoe heel wedged in between the planks of the floor. So she left it there and kept on running, tossing the other shoe in her haste. She barged into Robert's cabin and glared at him as he was strapping up his bag.

"What do you want?" he blurted in disgust. Maria's face showed beads of sweat, and her erratic breathing led Robert to surmise that she had changed her mind. "Don't you even think about it," he bellowed, grabbing her arm with his strong hand. Maria felt his fingers embedded into her soft skin.

"You're hurting me," she screeched. Robert grabbed his bag with one hand, and Maria with the other, and then quickly departed down the gangplank. Maria begged him to let her return to her cabin to get another pair of shoes, but he wouldn't, and her feet were sore and freezing. When they got to the street, Robert ushered a carriage and pushed her into it. Maria was even more frightened when he joined her, and he told the driver to take them to her address. The driver asked Maria if she was all right.

"You've been crying, miss?" he asked in a questioning, concerned voice. Before Maria was able to answer, Robert spoke up.

"She fell when we were leaving the ship. She's feeling much better now." The driver turned and proceeded silently.

Robert followed Maria up the long flights of stairs to the apartment she thought she would never see again. As she approached the old battered, dirty doorway, she began to weep.

"Please leave me now. I won't tell anyone about the money," she pleaded, wiping the tears from her face.

"Just open the door," Robert demanded.

Maria found her key under the doormat, but couldn't put it in the door, because her hands where trembling so wildly. Robert ripped it out of her hands and opened the door. He pushed Maria into the room and she tripped on her coat, landing on the floor of the dingy one room apartment. Her face was pressed against the hard, splintered floorboards. Robert began pulling at her coat.

"Give it to me," he demanded.

"Take it. Please go," Maria sobbed.

The coat came off and Maria, with her eyes shut tightly, kept her face pointed toward the floor, hoping to hear his footsteps leaving. But she didn't. She turned to look up, and to her horror, her worst fear was becoming an ugly reality.

"No! No!" she screamed until her voice went hoarse. She felt his big hands covering her mouth tightly. So tightly that she couldn't get enough air. Her skin crawled as he slowly lay on top of her. She could feel his hot smelly breath against her cheek. And his rough skin and beard scratched her pure white skin. She shut her eyes. And then instinctively, with her last remaining strength, her right knee jolted up to meet Robert's groin. He grunted, and punched her in the eye. It was a solid forceful impact and he heard a muffled thud when he hit her. A blood-curdling scream surfaced from deep inside, but never made its way out. She instantly lost consciousness. That's all she remembered. Maria didn't know whether she had remained unconscious, or if she had just blocked the rest of it out. The next thing she recalled was the door shutting.

Maria lay on the floor in a fetal position, hardly able to catch her breath from crying. Her head hurt. Badly. And she couldn't even think about standing. "I want to die," she cried. "I want to die!"

A New Start 3

Wilhelm had bathed and dressed and was waiting in the parlor to be called for dinner. Mr. Brunning had offered him his best cigar and he felt compelled to oblige, although he really didn't enjoy smoking all that much. The Brunning home was basked in rich burgundies and gold. Every fixture seemed to be made of the finest brass and the carpeting was of an oriental print. The curtains that draped from ceiling to floor were made of a heavy deep red, drawn back with golden tassels. A stunning grand piano sat in the corner of the room. And artwork of American presidents and Victorian themes were everywhere, surrounded by ornate gold-plated frames. The furniture was a mixture of fruit wood and mahogany and the detail on the drawers reminded Wilhelm of the furniture he had seen in Paris when he visited the city with his father as a boy. Wilhelm spotted a violin propped up in the corner of the room and picked it up. As he rubbed his hand over the smooth finish, he put the instrument up near his cheek, and then slowly and deliberately under his chin. The smell of the wood reminded him of home. He began to play a few notes at first, to get the feel of it. And then continued, completely submerging himself in the music, and forgetting where he was. Henrietta, the Brunnings' daughter, entered the room quietly. Wilhelm didn't see her come in. She was both stunned and mesmerized by the sight of this big handsome man, obviously making passionate love to the violin.

"You look as though you've left this earth," she said smiling. Wilhelm abruptly stopped as she had surprised him. "I'm sorry. I shouldn't have... Is this yours?" he asked.

"Oh please don't stop. I've never heard it played so beautifully. In fact, I've never heard anything ever played so beautifully," she cooed.

Henrietta was carefully dressed for dinner, in a frilly white and blue dress covered with bows and lace, with a big blue ribbon that wrapped around her waist and tied in the back with one more enormous bow. Her hair was curled, so that it fell down both sides of her face in large spirals, and it was held above her forehead by a large shiny pink ribbon. When Wilhelm stopped to look her over, he thought that there seemed to be too much of Henrietta to take in at once. Not that she was a large girl. In fact, she was quite petite. But there was such an overabundance of frill on every part of her body, she reminded him of an elaborate birthday cake that would make you feel sick after eating it. She quickly walked over to him, and Wilhelm couldn't help concentrating on how particularly close to his face she was whenever she spoke. She seemed to peer up at him... entranced. "Her eyes carry a glazed over look, and she smiles far too much," Wilhelm thought. Henrietta took the violin and bow out of his hands, placed them on the floor, and then proceeded to wrap his arm in hers and walked with him toward the dining room.

"Dinner is ready, and Mom asked me to escort you," she said, still gazing into his eyes.

As they entered the dining room, Mr. and Mrs. Brunning were already seated. Mr. Brunning sat, staring straight ahead, looking out of the window, as if he fantasized about being somewhere else. Mrs. Brunning was beaming, as she watched her daughter escort Wilhelm into the room.

"What a handsome couple you both make," Mrs. Brunning blurted. Both Wilhelm and Henrietta turned red, and looked at the floor as they sat down.

The meal was incredible. "We would only eat a meal like this on Christmas," Wilhelm complimented Mrs. Brunning. As Wilhelm glanced around the large dining room, he noticed that the color scheme continued into this room as well. Everything was perfect. Everything matched. Everything looked as if it was well planned and thought out. And that went for the meal, too. Wilhelm didn't know if he was just especially hungry, or if Mrs. Brunning was just a tremendous cook, but it was delicious, and he took extra helpings whenever they were offered. He remembered thinking that Henrietta ate a lot for a girl, and thought that she was sure to resemble her mother soon if she kept it up. He also noticed that Mr. Brunning had said roughly two words the entire evening. And then he recalled that in fact, he had only said a few words when he spoke with him on the ship. His thoughts seemed to be off in the distance somewhere far away.

After dinner, they all retreated into the parlor, and Mr. Brunning lit a fire. "Please play the violin," Henrietta pleaded.

Wilhelm was embarrassed at first, but with some persistent pleading, he agreed and picked it up. As he played, the Brunnings were silent. It was so beautiful that both Henrietta and her mother wiped tears from their eyes during certain passages. Wilhelm played on for hours, and the Brunnings sat motionless. Silent. Completely entranced by what they were witnessing. Wilhelm finally stopped, and told them he was quite tired. Mrs. Brunning slovenly hoisted herself up and escorted him to his room.

"You should be playing professionally with the New York Symphony," Mrs. Brunning gushed. "Honestly. I'm not just saying that. I know people who you can see. I'll arrange for it," she insisted.

Wilhelm retreated to the comfortable room. He had never been so tired. And by the time he awoke, it was 11:00 the following morning. He had been startled by a knock at the front door, and although his bedroom was upstairs, the heavy brass knocker seemed to shake the entire house. He jumped up and looked out the window. It was the police! "Why are they here?" he thought, with a panic starting to set in. Soon there was a knock at his door. It was Mr. Brunning.

"My wife has insisted that we have our friend at the police department come to see you in hopes that they can find you your money," he said shyly, knowing he was intruding.

"I'll be right down," Wilhelm replied.

Wilhelm quickly got dressed. His mind was turning and planning quickly, and he felt unsure that he could take care of the situation without raising suspicion.

"Mr. Brunning did say it was a friend though, so he wouldn't try to deport me," Wilhelm consoled himself.

He left his room and looked down the long winding staircase. At the foot of the stairs was Mrs. Brunning, dressed in a big blue dress with a matching hat, accompanied by a policeman in full uniform. Wilhelm noticed the officer's hand firmly wrapped around a large, black billy club, and he stopped to take a deep breath before walking down the stairs.

"Ah, this is our young man," Mrs. Brunning boasted, with a broad toothy smile. "Wilhelm, I want you to meet a friend of mine, Sergeant O'Rourke. Sergeant, may I present Wilhelm Strauss."

"Nice to meet you lad," the sergeant said with a smile, removing his hat. O'Rourke was a short, portly man with rosy cheeks, and sparkling blue eyes.

"He seems like a nice man," Wilhelm thought, a bit relieved.

"Mrs. Brunning has told me that you've been robbed of a thousand dollars your father had given you for living expenses. I'm here to fill out a report so that we can get working on finding the thief and get your money back to you," the sergeant said while walking over to sit on a large oversized chair in the parlor.

"Actually sir, it is not important. I don't want to make an issue of this. And I'm afraid I really don't know where the money is, or if it was even stolen," Wilhelm stuttered.

He was beginning to hyperventilate, and took a few deep breaths. He walked over to join the sergeant on a nearby couch. Mrs. Brunning followed so closely behind him that he could feel her warm, moist breath on his neck. She sat, facing Wilhelm. As he glanced up at her he noticed she was staring at him with one eyebrow raised. She looked angry, and confused. The sergeant began his questioning, immediately writing down Wilhelm's answers without looking up.

"The spelling of your last name is Strauss?"

"Yes, sir."

"And you're from what part of Germany?"

"Hanover Province, sir."

Now Mrs. Brunning began stirring in her chair, shifting her fleshy shapeless legs anxiously from side to side.

"And where was this money hidden?"

"In the lining of my trunk."

"And when did you first notice it was missing?"

"After I arrived in New York, I was looking through my bag, and I noticed it then."

A bead of sweat was slowly dripping down Wilhelm's forehead.

"Please don't ask me about my papers," he pleaded silently. Although O'Rourke continued to look down at his clipboard, Mrs. Brunning steadied her cold stare directly into Wilhelm's eyes.

"Was there anyone on the ship that you became friendly with? Anyone you may have shared the secret of your money with?" O'Rourke continued. Wilhelm paused. He remembered Maria, and his heart sank. He remained suspicious of her, but every time he thought about the possibility that she was involved, it hurt so much he pushed the thought out of his mind. He was still deeply in love with her, and he wanted to find her desperately.

"No," Wilhelm responded with calm assurance.

"I'm sorry son. My hearing's not what it used to be. Did you say, no?"

"No, I didn't meet anyone like that," Wilhelm said emphatically so O'Rourke could hear him. He didn't want to look up. But something made him, and Mrs. Brunning's stare had now turned to anger. It was clearly visible on her face.

"Perhaps you're forgetting Maria," she suggested.

"Maria wouldn't know of any of this. I know we saw a lot of each other, but we really didn't get very personal," Wilhelm responded.

O'Rourke looked up at both of them, and realized there was tension over the topic.

"Well, that's all I need now. Call me if you think of anything else that can help us,"

O'Rourke said as he put his hat back on and walked toward the door.

"Thank you, Bill. Give Eileen our love," Mrs. Brunning said graciously. When the door shut, Mrs. Brunning ambled up and peered out the window for a moment, and then catapulted around to Wilhelm.

"You're lying. And you told me you didn't know anyone from Hanover Province, so I know you're lying, but I don't know why," she said in a stern cold voice. Her face was beet red. Wilhelm squirmed in his chair. He could feel Mrs. Brunning's steely, silent stare. Her icy eyes felt as if they were ripping right through him.

"It's that girl. You're in love with her so you don't want her to get in trouble," she demanded in anger. Wilhelm looked up at her, and with his voice trembling, he said, "Mrs. Brunning, I am very grateful for your hospitality, and I would understand if you want me to leave." He paused, and then spoke softly.

"I don't want to leave this country. And I am

only supposed to be here for a short time on business. If you attract the police to me, or any more attention to me, there are bound to be questions, and I'll be deported."

Mrs. Brunning's knees buckled and she sat swiftly down on the couch. For several moments the room was encased in silence.

"Why didn't you tell me?" Mrs. Brunning blurted. "Mr. Brunning can arrange to have that taken care of. We have many friends in this city. All of them in high places," she said proudly, with her pug nose upturned toward the ceiling.

From that point on, the subject never resurfaced.

Several days passed and although Wilhelm wanted to find Maria, without any money he didn't have transportation. And he didn't dare approach the subject with Mrs. Brunning. Then it was arranged that Wilhelm would accompany Mr. Brunning to Chalfont's where he worked. Brunning, who was an executive of the store, had already spoken to the store manager about obtaining Wilhelm an entry-level job. They left the house that morning in their black suits and large heavy overcoats since the morning air was especially brisk. They could walk to Chalfont's as it was only several blocks away. Steam and smoke swirled in the air as they walked quickly against the wind. Mr. Brunning pulled a black billfold from his coat pocket.

"I've changed your name," he said calmly without missing a step. "Your last name is now King. You were born in New York City to parents who migrated from Germany, but they're dead now. This is what you will tell everyone at Chalfont's. And this is how you will live from now on. I don't know what trouble you were in over there, or what you're running from, but it's over now," he continued without even looking up. Wilhelm was in shock. He briefly looked at the wrinkled, frail man as he talked. He decided not to say a word in response. He too, kept walking.

"This is my chance at a clean start. I'll just accept this," he thought. He took the papers and stuffed them carefully into his pocket without further mention.

When they arrived, Wilhelm was introduced to the store manager, a Mr. Kean, and Mr. Brunning went on his way. As Mr. Kean took him around the store for a brief tour, Wilhelm felt instantly at home. This was the business he grew up around. "Although," he thought smirking, "this is quite a bit more fancy." They went behind the counters into a room in the back of the store, and Wilhelm could see that a supervisor was having a loud confrontation with a burly-looking employee.

"We're about to lose our best engraver," Kean whispered to Wilhelm. "And they're not easy to come by."

The burly man grabbed his coat and hat and rushed from the room, slamming the door abruptly behind him. Everyone present, looked at each other in puzzlement.

Out of the silence, Wilhelm cleared his voice and spoke up, "Mr. Kean, I am a qualified, and a very good engraver. My father, who is dead now, taught me how."

Kean's face lit up.

"Are you sure?"

"Yes. I'm sure I can do the job," Wilhelm said as he picked up a piece of jewelry the burly man was working on. He smiled at Kean.

"In fact, I can do it better."

Kean yelled gleefully to the supervisor, introduced Wilhelm as Brunning's boy, and they put him immediately to work. As the day was winding down, Kean called Wilhelm into his office to discuss salary.

"It's good pay," Wilhelm thought. "My life in America is on its way!"

The Meeting 4

A few days came and passed before Maria was able to pull herself together. The swelling around her eye had gone down, and she thought she would be able to cover most of her bruises with make-up. She bathed for a long time, scrubbing and scrubbing until her skin was raw. And in the morning she knew she had to get dressed and out to look for a job. She hadn't eaten anything since the attack, and she was beginning to regain her appetite. Morning came, and she went through her closet to find her most presentable dress. She found a gray wool suit dress that made her look matronly, but it was clean and not too worn, so she put it on. She pulled her hair back, and applied plenty of make-up, doing a very good job at hiding her injuries.

Standing in the corner of the dark room, she tried to gather herself together. She felt weak and dizzy from not eating, but her eyes were entranced by something sparkling in the corner of the room. Her heart raced as she ran over and slid on her hands and knees. It was a diamond earring. "It must have fallen out of my coat pocket!" she thought, elated by her find. She sat on the floor, clutching the diamond tightly in her hand and laughed out loud. She propelled up, and grabbed her pilled, worn, woolen coat and ran out of her apartment onto the street. The frigid air nearly took her breath away, but she walked briskly. She was smiling. "This is my first real true lucky break," she thought.

Maria walked and walked, through the dirty industrial neighborhoods and then toward Fifth Avenue. She wanted to return the jewel to the store where Robert bought it. She knew that would be her best chance at receiving top value. Although tired and fragile, she was determined to make it. She would stop in stores along the way, catching glares from store owners who knew she was getting in out of the cold. And she rested on benches whenever she could, hopefully next to a chestnut vendor, so that she could warm herself by the fire.

Finally, she had made it. "Chalfont Jewelers." As she walked through the etched glass doors of the opulent store, she felt as if the entire staff stopped dead in their tracks to gape at her. In fact, most of them were baffled by her. She was alarmingly beautiful. Regal looking, with her hair and make-up done the way Robert had taught her. But her clothes looked like a commoner and she was quite obviously battered and bruised beneath her shield of make-up. She walked directly up to the counter where the earrings were purchased and a stuffy balding man in a black suit looked up at her with his nose in the air.

"Can I help you?" he said doubtfully.

"Yes, thank you. I would like to return this. I've lost the other, and it's of no use to me."

The clerk looked at the earring she had placed in his hand. He looked up again at Maria, and then again at the jewel, in wonderment.

"Wait here please," he requested as he went into the back room.

There were audible sounds of commotion coming from the room. And Maria couldn't help noticing that employees were taking turns gawking at her through the small window in the door. She was embarrassed because she knew they were looking at her clothing and her swollen face, and she clutched her coat tightly to her breast. "Let them stare," she thought, as she kept her gaze no higher than counter level. She was about to have the money she would need to get her life on track. The clerk reappeared and asked her if she would like to purchase another match to the pair. Maria paused a moment, as if to think about it, and then declined. Kean was called over to inspect the transaction for final approval, and then he counted out the money to hand over to Maria. She stood with her palm upturned, waiting for him to finish.

"That will be $400, miss."

Maria's hand began to tremble uncontrollably as he handed her the money.

"Four hundred dollars?" Maria asked, as her mouth dropped open.

"Yes miss. Is there anything wrong?"

"No. No. There is absolutely nothing wrong," Maria responded with glee. She had no idea the jewel was that valuable.

Quickly placing the money into her pocket, she turned to leave, but glanced up first at the man peering at her from behind the door. To her astonishment, it was Wilhelm. The sight of him made her gasp for breath. She stood frozen in place. Wilhelm couldn't believe it was Maria at first. She looked so different. But when she remained motionless with eyes locked on him, he was certain it was her. He hurried to the counter. "Maria," he said as if still in disbelief.

"I didn't know how to find you. I have so much to explain. So much to tell you. Where are you living?" Maria asked, trying to catch her breath.

Wilhelm quickly wrote out his address and handed it to her. "My last name is King now," he whispered. She seemed to understand. He was shocked and confused by her appearance. She wasn't dressed at all like she was on the ship. Her accent was gone, and as he glanced at her face, he could see in the light that she was bruised. His boss was looking at him angrily, so he reluctantly retreated toward the back room, looking back at Maria with every other step.

"Please come see me," he pleaded before he closed the door.

A stunned Maria stood staring at the door for minutes. Then realizing everyone was looking at her once again, she abruptly turned and left the store.

She promptly stopped at a local restaurant and ate ravenously. This gave her the time and replenishment she needed to consider what she needed to do with her life. "I need to look the way I looked on the ship," she thought. "I was immediately respected. Immediately taken seriously." She left the restaurant and strolled down Fifth Avenue, eyeing all of the store windows until she found the dress she was looking for. And in a little, exclusive dress shop, she found it. A beautiful green satin dress. She went into the shop and asked the dressmaker if it was available in her size. The dressmaker, a boxy shaped woman with a sharply turned up nose, looked at her with a snobbish expression and asked, "Do you realize how much it is?"

Maria scowled, "No, how would I ? You haven't told me yet."

"It's forty dollars," she said, assuming Maria would leave the store embarrassed.

"Do you provide fitting?"

"Yes, miss," the dressmaker responded with new-found politeness. She brought Maria the dress in her size and Maria put it on.

"It fits you perfectly already," the dressmaker said, surprised.

Maria agreed. "I'll wear it. Do you have any coats?"

"No, we don't, but I can tell you where to go," she said, writing down an address on a piece of paper.

Maria took a carriage to the recommended furrier and bought a black mink coat that she wrapped herself in upon leaving the store. She tossed her old worn coat in a rusted trash can on the sidewalk. Her new coat felt so warm and soft, and gentlemen on the street were tipping their hats as she walked by. It was getting late and she retreated home to mend her bruised body and soul.

Three weeks had passed, and Maria's battered face had regained its natural beauty. She felt strong and self-assured. She had been thinking of Wilhelm since she saw him, and not much else. Taking a deep breath, she took out the address she had been so carefully holding onto, walked downstairs with newly found determination and asked a driver to take her there.

Upon arriving at the Brunnings, Maria was feeling lightheaded. She climbed the stairs carefully, holding on to the railing and knocked on the big ornate door. Mrs. Brunning opened the door and gasped in horror. This was the last person she wanted to see. But she managed to feign a broad forced smile. "Come in Maria," Mrs. Brunning said politely. "So nice to see you again," she continued.

Maria walked in, but could barely see. She was slowly blacking out. Trying to regain her composure, Maria took several steps into the foyer, but finally she fell to the floor. Mrs. Brunning instinctively put a pillow under her head, and ran outside for help.

"Get Doctor Stewart at once. It's an emergency!" she yelled to the carriage man. He gestured and trotted off. She scurried back into the house and brought Maria a glass of water. Maria wandered in and out of consciousness while Mrs. Brunning stood over her. Moments later the doctor arrived. Maria had come to.

"Would you give us some privacy, Mrs. Brunning?" the doctor asked.

Maria felt the doctor's cold pudgy hands poking and pushing on her stomach. "Are you married?" the doctor asked. "No," Maria responded, puzzled by the inquiry. The doctor's face turned calloused. Maria looked up at him in fear.

"What is it?"

"Have you skipped a normal menstruation period?" the doctor asked calmly.

"Yes doctor, but I've been ill, and I..." Maria paused. She looked into the doctor's judgmental eyes. His pupils seemed to dilate. And before he opened his mouth, she already knew what he was about to say.

"I believe you're pregnant," the doctor finally blurted in disgust.

Mrs. Brunning was listening intently from around the corner of the room and dropped the glass of water she was carrying. Without stopping to clean it up, she rushed into the parlor, her thighs pushing her big dress with a bustling, swishing sound as she walked.

"My dear, I'm glad you're feeling better. Now I have a carriage waiting and you should get home to get your rest immediately."

Mrs. Brunning grabbed Maria's arm and lifted her off the couch, ushering her quickly to the door, and down the stairs to a carriage that happened to be passing by. Maria was dizzy. She felt surreal, as if this was a beautiful dream gone bad. She watched Mrs. Brunning hurry back up the steps, thanking the doctor on his way out the door.

Maria sat in the carriage, stunned by the news. "It'll be a bastard!" she thought, and began to cry. All of her hopes and dreams of a future had just been shattered. She would be a social outcast. She could never tell Wilhelm. Never let him know she was pregnant. What would he think? The sights and sounds of the city seemed to blur past her as the driver took her on her way.

Wilhelm returned home to the Brunnings that evening feeling like he was on top of the world. Henrietta was waiting for him at the door with a big broad smile. Again, overdressed in pinks and blues, she immediately took Wilhelm's hat and coat and asked him to sit in the parlor, while she found him a cigar.

"She's constantly in my face," Wilhelm thought.

Then he heard the recognizable swishing sound of Mrs. Brunning approaching. She looked concerned. Her jaw was protruding.

Her eyes were smaller than usual. Like slits. And she sternly asked Henrietta to leave the room. Mrs. Brunning pulled up a small wooden chair and engulfed it as she sat down.

Wilhelm thought that there was trouble.

"My father has died. Or I've lost my job. Or, I'm being deported," he feared. Mrs. Brunning twisted her wrinkled neck to make certain Henrietta had left the room. Then it recoiled and she fixed her eyes onto Wilhelm.

"That whore was here today," she blurted.

"Whore?" asked a puzzled Wilhelm.

"Maria," responded Mrs. Brunning in anger.

"She's pregnant, and she says you're the father. She says she wants your money to support the baby," Mrs. Brunning said with her teeth clenched tightly.

"I made her leave. I made it clear you don't want to see her."

Wilhelm's heart sank as he listened. He had decided on his way home that he would marry Maria.

"But this baby is not mine," he said, just realizing that Mrs. Brunning may believe Maria.

Wilhelm felt as though his world had crashed once again. He sat silently, staring at the fire Henrietta had started in the fireplace.

"Who could the father really be?" he said, thinking out loud, trying to make some sense of the shocking news.

"I would imagine, just about anyone," Mrs. Brunning said with a callous sarcasm.

"Please excuse me ma'am," Wilhelm said as he got up to retreat to his room.

Wilhelm sat in his room, staring out the window, thinking.

"How could she do this? I thought she was in love with me! How could she sleep with someone else?" he thought. "Whore!" he shouted. "Whore!" he screamed. With the force of his forearm he cleared off the top of his chest of drawers. Brushes and shaving tools flew into the air and landed with sudden thuds and crashes onto the floor.

He refused to cry. And right now, he was too angry. Mrs. Brunning stood at the bottom of the stairs and peered up at the closed door of Wilhelm's room. A broad, content smile beamed across her face as she listened to his angst. "Accomplished," she thought to herself proudly.

Wilhelm fell asleep without dinner. He wasn't feeling up to it.

The next morning he awoke to the sound of a pound on the door. "What's he doing here?" he thought in horror when he saw O'Rourke standing outside the door. Mrs. Brunning let him in, and he stood with his ear pressed to the crack he had opened in the doorway. They seemed to be talking in a whisper. Sweat started to drip down his forehead as he strained to overhear them. He could only hear words. Words that didn't necessarily mean anything. He opened the door another inch and put his eye to the edge of the opening. He could see them standing in the foyer. O'Rourke had a serious expression on his face. Mrs. Brunning seemed to be pleading with him. Although Wilhelm couldn't hear her, he knew that tone of voice. She was asking a favor. O'Rourke turned and left, and Mrs. Brunning immediately peered at Wilhelm's door. She saw him spying on her.

Wilhelm backed away from the door, and shut it slowly, hoping she didn't notice.

Mrs. Brunning was pleased with his interest. She stopped for a moment, and thought, "This would be a good opportunity to work my little scheme." A broad mischievous smile plastered across her face. Wilhelm heard the familiar sounds of Mrs. Brunning making her way carefully up the stairs as she approached his room.

He answered her knock with an innocent sounding, "Good morning."

Mrs. Brunning looked pale. As if someone had died.

"Wilhelm, this is very serious," she said quietly. "O'Rourke says the Department of Immigration is on to you," she said looking at the ground, gulping her words as if she was about to cry. Wilhelm watched her in horror. His heart was beating faster and faster. So fast, that Mrs. Brunning could see it moving from outside of his shirt. "I have a plan," she said, her fat face lighting up like an overdecorated Christmas tree. Wilhelm looked up at her in anticipation and relief.

"You'll marry Henrietta. She loves you. And you love her. And we all wanted a longer courtship, of course. But I know you both couldn't bear the thought of losing each other," she unfolded her plan gleefully. Wilhelm was in shock. His chin fell open, as he watched Mrs. Brunning continue.

"We'll call our friend who is a minister, and we can have the ceremony right here, tonight," she continued.

"Tonight?"

"Unless of course, you would like to wait. I'm sure the immigration board won't wait. But if you would prefer to have some time to think it over..." she said with a smug, concerned expression. Wilhelm gulped and sat down on the corner of his bed, looking at the floor.

"Of course, I'll marry Henrietta," he said, after

a long pause. He thought about Maria and became enraged. "I'll marry Henrietta," he repeated, while looking up into Mrs. Brunning's dancing, impish eyes.

At the local station house O'Rourke stood in front of the almost exclusively Irish police squad, holding up a typed list of characteristics. He continued to read from the list. "Dark hair usually worn pulled back, a pretty woman with green eyes. She's pregnant. No husband," he announced, his eyes darting to the floor, in a show of disgust. "So be careful with her. Don't rough her up. Mrs. Brunning's quite positive she's got Mr. King's money. And she thinks she'll be back around their house, so we're to keep a close watch, and arrest her on the spot," he said in a gruff voice. "Mrs. Brunning's very concerned about her. And she doesn't want the girl near them. She just filled me in this morning. You know how the Brunnings are people who don't like trouble, so you can imagine, she's very concerned to be notifying me."

Ten Years Later 5

It was a cold day that lay heavy with a foggy drizzle. The kind of day that kept a chill inside you, no matter what you were wearing. Robert watched the cracks in the sidewalk pass underneath his boots as he walked home from school. He was a handsome boy. Obviously smart, and streetwise, even for an eight year old. Margie Cunningham followed him, giggling. She would stop giggling each time Robert turned to look at her. Margie was an annoying little brat with reddish frizzy hair and freckles. Robert would sometimes sit in school during reading assignments and daydream about using his pen to connect the dots on her face. He would imagine different patterns he could create. A dog, a cat, even an automobile. As he sat gazing at Margie in class, she would look up at him and smile. She was sure he was as in love with her, as she was with him.

"Ouch!" Robert yelled with disgust as he turned around to see the face full of freckles almost pressed up against his. "You stepped on my heel," he reprimanded.

"Sorry," Margie giggled, as she dropped back a few steps. Robert looked up and spotted his brother Bill walking several yards ahead of him. He began running as fast as he could.

"Bill," he yelled. "Wait up."

Bill was the most popular kid in the school. And at nine years of age, he looked and acted at least five years older. Bill was also handsome, and much taller than most of the kids in his grade. Both boys had their father's strong, handsome features and wavy black hair. Bill's eyes were just as blue as his father's. Robert's were a blue-green. As they walked up the street lined with beautifully manicured lawns and large homes, they looked like miniature fighter pilots dressed in brown leather bomber jackets.

The driveway leading to their home was covered with white stones that Wilhelm had imported from Italy, and the willow trees that lined the property shielded the boys from the drizzle. The house sat up on a slight hill. It was a pretty white colonial style house with blue awnings on each of the windows. And in the spring, there was a patch of wildflowers in the middle of the lawn that burst with color on a sunny day. Wilhelm would often say " I'll spare no expense for my family." And the house was evidence of this. The King's house was surrounded by people of prominence. People in government, in show business, and high society.

The boys would let themselves in, because Henrietta wouldn't get home from her job in Manhattan until 6:00 or so. It wasn't that she had to work. She wanted to. She was quite a successful designer with Vogue patterns. And she enjoyed the celebrity of being involved in the fashion industry. Wilhelm hated that she worked. He made well in excess of what the family needed to live comfortably, and Henrietta's job was a source of embarrassment for him and the boys, especially since she was the only neighborhood mother who wasn't at home. But in Henrietta's world, Henrietta came first. And this is what she wanted to do. Wilhelm's schedule was a bit more flexible. He had worked as a jeweler at Chalfont's and moonlighted as a concert violinist on occasion, and had saved and invested his money wisely. A killing he made in the stock market gave him the advantage he needed to open his own company, and so even though he knew nothing about the industry, he bought an iron works that was for sale. Within two years the business was booming, and his building took up a full town block. He would typically shift his schedule around to get home by 4:00 so that the boys wouldn't be left too long in the house alone. And it was clear to anyone who knew the Kings, Wilhelm was the energy that kept the family together.

There was no stronger love than the love that Wilhelm felt for his boys. Everyone knew that. Robert was particularly close to him, and unnaturally distant from his mother. Bill, on the other hand, although he loved his father, seemed to gravitate toward his selfish mother. Most likely because he shared some of the same personality traits. Robert was clearly the smarter of the two boys. Bill was the more charismatic. They sat reading comic books, taking breaks to wrestle and tease each other. Between them they shared a strong bond. Because they were left on their own a lot, they were all each other had. Robert looked up to Bill. And Bill protected Robert.

"How are my guys today?" asked Wilhelm with a toothy grin as he walked in the door.

Just as handsome as ever, Wilhelm looked more distinguished the older he grew. His success showed in the way he dressed and moved. And most people felt instantly in awe of his presence. He was carrying bags of food from the store, and he lay them down on the kitchen table. Sweeping his hand into a drawer, he grabbed a frilly apron and wrapped it around his waist. It was not an unusual sight, to see Wilhelm cooking dinner. It was also not unusual to see him pour himself a good stiff glass of Scotch. There was a sadness in his eyes, and often the boys would catch him staring into space. As if he were in some other place, some other life.

At 6:15 the back door swung open. "What's for dinner?" Henrietta asked with an enthusiastic smile as she walked in. The years had not been as kind to Henrietta. Wilhelm had convinced her to get pregnant, as the thought of raising a family wasn't the most important thing on her agenda. And Wilhelm had often thought that she was paying him back by continuing to look pregnant for good, after Robert was born. He often thought about how much she looked like her mother when he met her on the ship that first night. Fat and overbearing. Mrs. Brunning had passed away last year, as did Henrietta's father the year before. Now Wilhelm and the boys were all she had. And Wilhelm, although he had tried to contact his father to no avail, had no one either.

"A match made in heaven," Wilhelm would often think sarcastically while pondering their mutual loneliness.

He held a simmering hatred for Henrietta way down deep in his gut. And he covered it up each night under a layer of Scotch. He resented everything she was about. He resented having to marry her in the first place. And he hated her selfishness. Often, he would still think of Maria, after all these years. He had heard she was working in show business in California. But there was far too much mistrust and hatred to even think of contacting her. Yet he was curious as to what she was doing and how she was, and he had an enormous list of unanswered questions for her.

"Hi Mom!" the boys cheered in unison.

"How was your day?" Wilhelm asked as he noted an expression on her face that seemed unfamiliarly pleasant.

"My day? My day was wonderful," she sang. "You are looking at the new chief designer."

"Hurrah!" the boys yelled, their big white teeth sparkling.

"Hurrah," replied Wilhelm in a low sarcastic monotone, raising his Scotch into the air as if to offer a toast.

"Of course, it will mean I'll be working a few more hours a week, but just look at this salary!" She handed Wilhelm a piece of paper.

The boys watched her as she danced around the kitchen with a proud happy look on her face. At one point, she grabbed the broom from the closet and swaggered around the room as if she were in a ballroom with a mysterious lover. Robert couldn't help thinking of last week when he showed her his report card. Straight A's. "Mom will be proud of me for this," he had thought. Instead, he received a lukewarm, "Congratulations" accompanied by a quick peck on the cheek.

"After dinner, we really need to discuss the Florida deal" she demanded as she shot Wilhelm a serious look.

"OK, yes. Between the two of us, we certainly need to plan our investments carefully now," Wilhelm reservedly responded.

"Carefully isn't the word. We're downright rich!" Henrietta bragged, looking to the boys for their excited approval.

The boys ate swiftly that night because they knew they should retreat to their rooms whenever Mom and Dad were about to talk money.

"May I be excused?" asked Bill.

"Me too?"

"Yes, by all means. Make sure you finish your homework before you start fooling around," demanded Wilhelm.

As the boys left the room, Henrietta's eyes fixated on Wilhelm's glazed-over stare.

"Wilhelm, let's talk about this before you have your next glass of Scotch," she demanded.

"It's fine Henrietta. I'll call Ed Williams tomorrow. It's a risky investment, to put all of our money in one place, but Ed agrees with you. He feels we'll double our savings in a matter of a few years."

"It's not risky," blurted Henrietta. "Florida real estate is booming. It's a favorite vacation spot for all of our friends. And this is an extremely large, professional development corporation. Ed says he's invested heavily himself. And I'm sure he wouldn't steer us in the wrong direction."

"I'm not fighting with you. I'll do it tomorrow,"

Wilhelm responded flatly. Henrietta looked up at Wilhelm. His beautiful blue eyes were glazed over with a drunken calm. She was still in love with him, and it hurt her deeply to feel that the love wasn't reciprocated.

"I'm tired. I'm going up to bed now," Wilhelm announced. Henrietta followed him up the stairs.

As Wilhelm began to undress, Henrietta quietly walked over to her vanity table and pulled out the pins that held her long blonde hair up in place. This was her nightly ritual, to brush her hair with at least a hundred strokes. Quietly she got up and walked over to get in the bed.

She lay thinking about their relationship. "Why did he marry me if he didn't love me?" she thought, choking back her tears of self pity. She thought about the years he was fighting in World War I, about the daily letters she would send him. Only to receive one every month or two. Her letters were filled with passion. His were filled with questions, mainly about the boys, the house and the business. She worried about his safety every waking moment. He missed the boys. Her fist hit the bed next to her as she began to grow angry. Wilhelm snored.

"Why? Why did you bother with me? Why did you marry me?" she cried under her breath. "I love you," she cried out in desperation. Wilhelm continued to snore. Henrietta recalled how she buried herself in her work, to avoid any free time that she could focus on how little love Wilhelm showed her. The accolades she received for her talent was the only form of love she received. Except for the love of her boys. "But that doesn't really count," she thought. "That's an unconditional love. Every child loves their mother. I need someone to love me because I'm special. And that's what happens at work. They love me there. I'm important there. Not because they have to. But because I'm talented." She fell asleep while deep in thought.

Wilhelm got up quite early that morning to get into the factory. A stark, plain light bulb hung down over his head as he sat at his gray steel desk. The only hint of warmth in the room appeared on his swivel chair, which was cush-ioned with a soft comfortable pillow that Henrietta had stuffed for him. His phone was busy constantly, but his most important call was placed first thing to Ed Williams, his stock-broker. Wilhelm had done very well playing the market, and this was about to be his biggest, most risky investment. "Ed, how are you?"

"Just fine Wilhelm, how are Henrietta and the kids?"

"Oh, fine, thanks. Listen Ed, we're ready to put all our free cash into that Florida development firm you recommended."

"Excellent move, Wilhelm. You won't be dis-satisfied. We're all making quick money on this one! Just get me a check this afternoon and I'll take care of it for you."

That evening, when Henrietta came home, she danced into the doorway again. "We're in the money, we're in the money!" she sang as she clapped her shoes above her head. The kids smiled as they looked up from their dinner plates at their jubilant mom. "You did buy it, right?" she paused, waiting for Wilhelm to respond.

"I bought it, at 12:30 this afternoon. I bought it at 13," boasted Wilhelm.

"Thirteen?" shrieked Henrietta gleefully. "It's already at 14 1/2!"

"I know."

Henrietta ran over to Wilhelm and kissed him on the cheek. He smirked and turned slightly red, obviously proud of his accomplishment.

"Are we rich, Mom?" asked Robert.

"We were rich. Now we're swimming in it!" she shrieked.

Three days later, the boys awoke to the surprise of their lives. "No school today boys," Wilhelm declared just as they were racing to the breakfast nook. The boys stopped dead in their tracks.

"Why not?" Bill asked.

"Because we're going on a little trip to celebrate!" Henrietta screeched.

Wilhelm opened up the back door to display a brand new baby blue colored Cadillac. He had a proud look on his face as the boys yelled their enthusiastic approval. They ran out to see the new chrome covered car sparkling in the sunlight. Robert glanced back and noticed Wilhelm had his arm around Henrietta. This was a sight he hadn't seen in years. They were all the happiest they had ever been that day. The stock had continued to rise dramatically and had reached 20 per share!

Bill and Robert were fervently exploring every square inch of the new car.

"Where are we going?" Bill asked from the back seat where they had already assumed comfortable positions.

"We're driving down to see our property in Florida. It's near Miami Beach. You'll need to pack all of your summer clothing. So, get a move-on," Henrietta announced in a seemingly stern, yet playful voice.

"Florida!" they yelled.

As the boys ran upstairs, Wilhelm looked at Henrietta. "I've been hard on her" he thought.

"I'm not in love with her, but I do care for her. There's a difference. And basically, although she's selfish at times, she's a good person."

At that moment Henrietta looked up into his eyes and smiled softly. For the first time, she felt a warmth from Wilhelm she had never seen before. She slapped him on the backside. "And that goes for you too," she said jokingly.

"I'm going. I'm going," he responded with a smirk as he turned to head up the stairs.

What a vacation it was! No expenses were spared. They stayed in only the finest hotels, ate in the finest restaurants, saw the best of shows and only talked to the wealthiest of people. The entire family remarked constantly at how beautiful Florida was, and how pristine a setting the land was that they had invested in. Sugar white sand, surrounded by swaying green palm trees, and aqua blue water. Wilhelm would never forget the look on Robert's face as he screamed from the water in ecstasy, "This is as warm as a bathtub!" They stopped in Palm Beach and went shopping in some of the most exclusive stores they had ever seen. Everything was white and bright and full of sparkling color. Wilhelm remembered thinking that they seemed like a real family for the first time. Together, and enjoying each others' company. There was even a night when the boys were asleep in bed that he and Henrietta went for a moonlight stroll on the beach. It was a beautiful warm, humid night and the moonlight lit up her hair. A soft glow accented the pretty features that still appeared on her face. They were passionate that night. And the next morning they woke up giggling with each other like school children.

Finally, one morning, Wilhelm called into the office to receive news that there was a problem with a piece of equipment. They would have to cut the vacation short and head back to New Jersey.

"We've been here long enough to heal some of the wounds we've all been feeling," said Henrietta gently when Wilhelm told her they'd have to return.

He smiled and agreed.

The morning Wilhelm returned to the office he got in early, before anyone else had arrived.

He was concentrating on the paperwork regarding the repair of equipment. Employees were arriving, one by one. Yet, Wilhelm had an eerie sense about the day. It seemed chilly in the dark, gray room. Quiet. And still. His secretary smiled and waved to him through the glass. She mouthed the words "Welcome back," smiled, and took her sweater off before sitting down.

Suddenly, out of the stillness, the phone rang so loudly that it sent a chill up Wilhelm's spine.

His secretary announced, "Mr. King, there's an urgent call from Ed Williams for you. Do you want to take it?"

"Sure, I'll talk to him quickly."

He picked up the phone.

"So Ed, are you swimming in it?" he said jokingly.

"Wilhelm, have you heard the news?"

Ed's voice was shrill and vacant. It was a desperate voice that Wilhelm had never heard before from him.

Wilhelm took a deep breath.

"Ed. Calm down. What news? What's wrong? Did our stock take a little dip?"

There was silence. A silence that seemed endless.

Wilhelm took another deep breath. "Ed, all stocks take a little dip now and then," he said positively.

"Wilhelm, I'm sorry."

"Ed. Are you crying?! Ed. What the hell is wrong!?" he screamed.

There was silence.

"Ed. What is wrong?!"

Wilhelm sat quietly, listening.

Ed's hand must have been over the phone. But he could hear sobbing. Muffled sobbing. Then more silence. Eerie silence.

Then… a gunshot.

"Ed. Ed!"

"Edith," he yelled. "Get me the police!"

Edith immediately got the police on the phone, and Wilhelm frantically explained his conversation with Ed Williams. He got up from his chair and began pacing his office.

The light bulb that hung over his desk swung from left to right, sending a diabolic cast of shadows into movement across his office.

Sweat was rolling down his forehead. He felt desperate, unsure of what was happening.

Suddenly the plant manager, Pat O'Casey, burst into his office.

"Wilhelm, the stock market has crashed!"

"What do you mean, crashed?" he asked, his voice quivering.

"I mean, everyone in this building has fled from their jobs to run to the bank. The radio is saying that there's no money left in the stock market, and the banks are all running out too!"

Pat's shirt was soaked through with perspiration. "You have to help me Wilhelm. Everything I own is in First Fidelity!"

His face contorted as he spoke.

Wilhelm could see by his reaction that this was no minor emergency. He grabbed his coat and hat and ran out of the office, leaving Pat without a word of consolation.

Star Light. Star Bright. 6

Maria gargled with champagne quietly to wash the taste of last night's alcohol from her mouth. She gripped the satin sheets tightly around her as she slowly propped herself up in the bed. She had been awakened by a loud knocking at her door. When she opened the door, she was surprised to find David waiting for her. A smelly cigar hung from his sagging fat lips, and he stared at her, as if he thought he was seducing her with his swollen, fleshy eyes.

"Ugly, smelly pig," she said under her breath.

"I've got a part for you kid," he bragged as he plopped himself onto her living room couch.

"For me?" Maria acted surprised.

"I know you've only been in one film. But you got quite a bit of attention. And I think you have star appeal. I'm going to try you out."

"What's the picture?" Maria asked, truly excited now.

"Tapestry."

"Tapestry? Tapestry!!?" Maria shrieked with delight. "That's the hottest property out there right now!"

"That's right. So, I'm taking a gamble. And I'll assume you won't let me down."

David looked at her and smirked.

She had daydreamed about starring in "Tapestry."

"The book was excellent. Will I be Laura?" she asked, suddenly worried she had misunderstood.

"No, you'll play the maid," David responded seriously.

Maria looked up at him with disappointment, and then realized he was teasing her.

She laughed as David winked his bloated eye.

He walked over to her, and still huffing and gasping, he lunged over and pinched her backside before leaving.

With another sarcastic wink, he said, "A car will be here any minute to take you to the studio for a screen test. Try to look presentable."

She watched quietly as his big rubbery rear edged out the door.

When the door slammed, she jumped up and walked over to the mirror. She removed her clothes and draped a bed sheet around her white flawless skin, and stood for a while, admiring her image. She swirled the sheet around her, and it flew gracefully into the air. The sunlight made her green eyes glisten. She waltzed around the room, stopping to sip champagne now and again.

"I can play a French mistress better than anyone. I've already done it, for months, quite convincingly, on a ship, no less!" she gloated to herself.

She stopped to glance out of her apartment

window as David's driver pulled away. A little blonde haired girl in a pink frilly dress was jumping rope on the sidewalk just below. A horrible, empty feeling overcame her. She stood, transfixed on the girl. She thought about her baby, Jenny. And she wondered, "Is she starting to look like her movie star mom, or her savage, ape of a father?" For all she knew, this little girl down on the sidewalk was her own daughter. Just as that thought emerged, the little girl's mother came out to wrap a coat around her shoulders, and with a quick hug, she gave her a gentle kiss on the cheek. Maria's eyesight focused again. "Snap out of it! You've just received the best news of your life, and you're going to ruin it by thinking about Jenny again?" she scolded herself.

As she wiped the tear off her cheek, her thoughts were interrupted by the sound of a large chrome covered car beeping its horn below. A chill sent a shiver through her body and she quickly rebounded her excitement.

"A screen test!" she yelped, and jumped up in the air, her champagne dribbling out onto the cushioned, powder blue carpet. She ran over to her white closet door and twisted the ornate crystal handle.

"What should I wear? Something really revealing. Something that says I'm a French maid. Something that says I am a movie star, so don't even think about not giving me this part!"

She found a slinky red dress with a bit of fringe around the bottom, that would shimmer when she walked. And then she cast her silky, firm legs in black fishnet stockings with a seam running up the back. To top it off, she squeezed her feet into very tall, thin, high-heeled shoes with a sharp point at the toes. A ruby and diamond necklace completed the picture. She stopped to assess herself in the mirror as she began to brush her disheveled hair.

"It's wild," she thought, as she put her fingers through her thick black mane. "That's right. Wild!" A creative spark ran through her brain. "And wild, it will be!" she said out loud as she puffed her hair even more. "I'll bet nobody has walked in for an audition looking like this!" she thought proudly.

She answered a knock at her door, and a small

mustached man in a gray uniform stood smiling.

"Are you ready, miss?" he asked politely as his eyes wandered up and down the incredible woman standing before him.

"Ready," Maria said confidently, tossing her hair behind her as she turned to lock the door. The ride to the movie studio was filled with sights. New shiny cars. Women dressed up in fine whites and pastel blues and pinks. Their hair all neatly hidden beneath elaborate hats with wide brims to block the sun. The homes were extremely modern, and were typical of the new California style that was all the rage.

"Miss Maria Cardone is here to see Mr. Semple," the driver said, and the man at the gate saluted, first to the driver, and then with a tip of his hat and a raise of his brow, to Maria.

The driver saw Maria to Mr. Semple's secretary and then left. "A mousy little number," Maria thought to herself, completely unimpressed. Maria stood and took a deep breath before walking through the door Mr. Semple's secretary had just opened. She slinked around the corner of the door and concentrated on moving every part of her body as she walked. The short, fat, balding man behind the huge cherry wood desk sat up from his slumped position, and lowered his glasses to the tip of his nose. The room smelled of stale cigar smoke and Maria's first thoughts were that he was a little sweet man. A gentle man.

"Your name is fine. You can keep it," he said hastily.

"My name? I never even thought of changing my name," Maria responded, shocked that it was even under consideration.

He stood up and walked around the desk toward Maria, his eyes not blinking as he stared into hers.

His face began to contort with anger. "Let's get something straight right now. You are not supposed to think. You follow my explicit direction. And you do precisely what I say. Do you understand?"

He was now standing directly over her.

Maria cowered, "Yes, all I meant was..."

He cut her off. "Follow me to the screening room," he said, flashing a warm smile that again made him appear like someone's comfortable father.

Maria's life itself was probably more interesting than the Tapestry plot. Having been born and raised in Brooklyn in a lower class neighborhood, her friends and classmates had experienced it all by the age of 15. Death. Murder. Parents' adulterous affairs. Pregnancy. And theft. It permeated the neighborhood. Yet her household had none of that. Her father and mother were good Catholics. Her father, an Italian immigrant, worked in a local hosiery factory. And her mother, whose ancestors were Irish, was a housewife. She was devoted to Maria and her brother, as well as to Maria's father, who tended to drink a bit too much on occasion. However, Maria wanted more. And she was well aware that she had the "looks" to make it all happen for her. Maria had moved back home to Brooklyn when she learned she was pregnant. And so, as not to shame her family, she mostly remained indoors, unless her stomach was disguised with a full sweater or coat. It worked. In fact, nobody in the neighborhood ever found out she was pregnant. Several days before the baby was due, she and her brother, posing as husband and wife, stayed in a fleabag motel close to the hospital. When the baby was born, it had already been arranged through her father's connections that a couple in Manhattan, who had been trying to have a baby for years, would come to take the newborn the day she was released from the hospital. Maria had fallen deeply in love with her new daughter from the second she first laid eyes on her, and letting go was the most difficult thing she had ever done. On the outside, it appeared easy to all of the people around her. But on the inside she was desperate and heartbroken. And because she would never share or show her grief, she felt even more isolated from her family. So she quickly moved out, and found herself a job modeling nude for an up-and-coming artist. It was here that she was discovered by a talent agent, through a connection that the artist had. As tough and progressive as Maria pretended to be on the surface, she was actually a nice Catholic girl who was ashamed of her past. In fact, she actually considered herself a virgin, since her one and only sexual experience was through a rape. This was not, however, the image she intended to project for the benefit of her career. And there was one overriding power for Maria. A power more forceful than family, friends or life itself. Money. Maria would do anything for money. She would do anything to escape the kind of life she grew up with. However, she was a walking dichotomy. And every time she did something for money, her guilt resurfaced.

Hitting a Wall 7

A silver wind chime sounded off in the silence of the warm summer night. Wilhelm sat motionless on the front porch, waiting for a call from Pat O'Casey. He stared out at the quiet calm of his backyard, and although he felt destitute and alone, he found some solitude in his temporary isolation. A fly buzzed around the naked light bulb overhead. "All my work is gone. It's all gone," he murmured to himself over and over. He took another quick gulp of the brandy that swirled around in his glass with every movement. Suddenly his remorse turned to anger. He walked down the hallway to the living room and rummaged through the old wooden desk in the corner.

There, stuffed into a false molding, well-hidden and camouflaged, were his Florida property bonds. Entitled, "Heavenly Sun Bonds," they looked very different now. No longer were they graphically designed to depict wealth, health and prosperity, but instead, they represented his very demise. "Worthless!" he cried out as he headed down to the basement. He tried to keep his composure. Although Henrietta and the children were asleep, he didn't dare let his true feelings surface. They were too strong. Too raw. And too overpowering to face them now. He quietly took a dusty bottle down from a shelf overhead, and proceeded to pour the gold colored glue out of the container onto the worktable set up in the corner. With stable hands he brushed one bond after the next, carefully coating the backs until they were thoroughly covered. The first one went up on the wall smoothly. And so did the next, and the next. Beads of sweat began to pour down his face as he took another swig from his glass. His movements started to become more and more frantic as he smoothed every bond securely covering the wall. "Worthless," he repeated without pause. As he smoothed yet another bond across the rough stucco wall the bond ripped and he had trouble securing it. He yanked it off and with violent motion began pasting and then pounding the tattered paper to the porous surface with little success. "Worthless. Worthless," he bellowed. Finally, with the scraps in his hand, his knees buckled to the floor. His hands were bleeding and left a crimson trace of blood against the wall as he sank. "Worthless. Worthless," he began to sob. Suddenly he was startled by the sound of a gasp. It was Robert, standing in the doorway, tears filling his eyes. He was gasping for breath. "Dad are you alright?" he stuttered, taking a short breath in between each word. Wilhelm's eyes fixated on Robert's, as if they were bringing him back from the brink of insanity. He quickly wrapped a towel around his bleeding hand and ran over to Robert. Landing on his knees in front of the boy, he flung his arms around him, holding him tightly, and didn't let go. Wilhelm felt cocooned in his son's love, and as long he held on tightly, no harm could come to him. He struggled to regain his composure and took deep breaths to avert his compulsion to cry.

Robert buried his head into his father's chest. He had never seen his Dad upset, even in the slightest, and this was a moment he would never forget for the rest of his life. It represented both deep pain and unsurpassed love all in one.

Wilhelm held Robert's hand as he led the boy back to his bedroom. He sat on the edge of the bed, and suggested that together they say the Lord's Prayer. They said the prayer in unison, Wilhelm's voice cracking every now and then. After Robert fell asleep, Wilhelm walked slowly toward his own bedroom. He was startled by Henrietta, who was standing at the doorway. Her eyes were transfixed on Wilhelm, and they were welled with tears. Wilhelm stopped suddenly as he noticed her. She looked beautiful. Money and success had taken very good care of her. She was wrapped in a powder blue satin bathrobe that draped on the floor behind her like a wedding gown train. And as she stood motionless with only the movement of the light sparkling on her eyes, her long flowing blonde hair streamed gently down the side of her strong, wholesome face. Clearly, Henrietta had become prettier as she aged. Her skin was flawless, and there was a purity and freshness to her features that seemed to illuminate from the caring person she had become within. She lifted her arms up to motion Wilhelm that she wanted to hug him, as he had seen her do with the boys to console them when they were hurt. Wilhelm ran to her, and falling to his knees, he hugged her waist and buried his face in her soft robe. They remained there silent for what seemed to be a good hour, as Henrietta stroked his head. Then she reached down and grabbed his hand and led him to their bed. Once in bed she cradled her soft body around his, and they stayed positioned that way for the entire night. A shred of light pierced Wilhelm's squinted eye in the morning, and he opened both eyes to look at Henrietta's face. She was still asleep, but as he watched her, he thought about how much he had come to love her. She had changed. Not only had she grown prettier with time, but she was strong and self-assured, yet feminine and beautiful. Those traces of her mother's personality that he despised, had vanished. "Henrietta," he said softly. Henrietta opened her eyes to look up into his. "I've been thinking all night. I need to contact my Dad."

Henrietta was surprised. He had not spoken of his father for years. He went on, "Last night, Robert came downstairs to comfort me during a time when I needed it most, and I often wonder what has become of my father. I had tried contacting him right after we were married and I was no longer fearful of deportation. And I don't know what stopped me from persevering. I guess I was afraid that he was dead, and that my leaving the country had been the cause. I just couldn't face that. But I need to know. I need him. Today I have to face all of the employees to tell them that we're bankrupt," he choked out the words. Henrietta stroked the back of his head as he spoke. "And knowing the comfort that Robert and Bill feel in my embrace, I need to feel that again with my own father, if it's still possible." Henrietta smiled.

"I'll help you in any way I can," Henrietta responded warmly. She looked down and then back up into Wilhelm's tired eyes. She grasped his hand and held it tightly. "We'll make it, you know," she said with confidence. "I haven't lost my job, and I'm making more than most husbands make today. And I understand that we're opening a new division that they're thinking of having me head. It's a chance of a lifetime for a designer. We're going after contracts with the major motion picture studios to represent certain stars. If I get this job, I'll be designing clothes for Clark Gable and Claudette Colbert." Henrietta was giddy with childlike enthusiasm. Wilhelm smiled and felt somewhat reassured. "It's my turn," she said softly, her eyes welling with emotion. "You've worked so hard. You've gotten us where we are today. Now it's my turn to do my part. Don't worry." Henrietta continued to stroke his head, as she dreamed of the possibilities of her new career.

Photo Play 8

A warm breeze floated across Maria's face as she lay reading a magazine poolside at the Beverly Hills Hotel. She had moved into the hotel while filming "Tapestry" which was almost ready to wrap. It had been an exhausting process, but a rewarding one. She had been signed onto a contract to be the next MGM starlet, and she would never have to worry about money again. She watched a puff of smoke as it swirled across the sky from her cigarette, and gently sailed by the white brim of her hat. She sat up for a moment to re-tie the long pink scarf that delicately draped from the hat to her soft chiseled chin.

Through the plush green bushes that were garnished with white gardenias, Maria heard the noises of families and old tired men waiting for the food lines to open. Maria closed her eyes and turned her head. She was annoyed that the hotel and the city would allow such a thing right outside of her home. She opened her Photoplay magazine and began to refocus her attention. Once again she was distracted by the cries of a little girl just outside the fence. She was a frail little thing. Pale and skinny with deep set eyes and dark circles below them. Her father was holding the tattered little girl, and wiped tears of hunger away from her dirt-smudged face. Maria winced, and packed up her bag in disgust. "Sure, it's a horrible thing," she thought to herself. "But I've come from a worse situation, and they have to help themselves. I have no sympathy." Her sight darted back to the little girl who now had a good portion of a hard roll in her mouth. Maria thought she looked like a wolf, as she quickly devoured every last crumb. "Disgusting," she said under her breath, as she headed for the entrance to her cottage. Once inside the pastel colored interior, drenched with the perfume of freshly cut gardenias, she helped herself to a single, plump chocolate that remained on a silver platter near the living room couch. Thirsty from the heat, she washed it down with a gulp of what was an endless stream of champagne that was delivered to her room every day. Wrapping an oversized terry cloth robe around her, she plopped down on the large billowy couch and began reviewing her final scenes in the "Tapestry" script.

The filming seemed endless, yet satisfying. And Maria was attended to the way she had always desired. The studio had very carefully paid off her family to keep quiet, and to Hollywood insiders, she had been raised on the upper east side of Manhattan by wealthy parents. There was to be no further information released about her. This was all at Maria's request. Although studio executives knew nothing of the specifics of her past, they had an inkling that everyone should keep it that way. Safe and secret. And Maria was well aware that if anyone ever found out about her unwed pregnancy, it would surely be scandalous enough to end her career. Maria had hired one of Hollywood's top agents, Sam Shell, and he wheeled and dealed with the tough Semple, at MGM. That left Maria out of the range of fire. And although the public was still virtually unaware of Maria's existence, both Shell and the studio knew it was only a matter of time. The buzz was strong. Louella Parsons had been present at the sound studio one day and declared in her column that Maria was "a woman on fire, with the classic beauty of a Greek goddess and the smoldering sensuality of a volcano ready to erupt." And the anticipation of "Tapestry" was at a fever pitch, with newspapers prophetizing it to be the biggest film in cinema history.

On the set, Maria drudged up every deeply hidden emotion she had. She was a true professional, and knew every line before she walked onto the set. Her co-star, Barry Anderson who was the #2 box office draw next to Clark Gable, was impressed with her. And he would often visit her trailer. Together, they would sip champagne between takes and routinely Barry would attempt to fondle Maria, but she would only let him get so far before cutting him off cold. This left him obsessed, and he would often leave the company of his wife and children who visited him on the set to join Maria in her trailer. Naturally, he told his wife they were rehearsing, but everyone on the set surmised there was something else going on. They were only half-way correct.

Just as Maria had finished reading her last line, there was a knock at the door. It was her driver. "We're ready for you, Miss Cardone." Maria hopped into the car, still in her bathrobe and the driver took her to wardrobe where they dressed her in a backless, tapestry print dress that was cut short, even by 1929 standards. It was her final scene, and she was determined to make it her best.

Six months later, Maria slithered down a red carpet, arm and arm with her co-star, amongst flashbulbs and screams from a multitude of fans who had surrounded the theater for opening night. She was dressed in the very same tapestry dress. Following the close of the movie, the audience sprang to their feet and applauded for a solid ten minutes. Maria felt happier and more in control than she ever had in her life. It was all like a dream come true. She and her co-star took a bow from the front row of the theater and the audience roared its approval.

Semple decided that Maria should travel the country, to make a special appearance in front of audiences in advance of the movie showing. Maria obliged, and decked out in scandalous outfits, she prowled out from behind a curtain and told racy jokes. The result of her tour and the overwhelming success of the film at the box office left Maria in the middle of a kaleidoscope of accolades and protests to her dirty act. In any case, she quickly became a household name, and a synonym for the word "sex." Yet, her publicity agent made it very clear that Maria was actually quite chaste, and was not a sexually active person. This was a necessary image to uphold. The public would embrace a sizzling sex symbol on the screen, but it was unwilling to forgive actual, personal sin.

She dated often, slept with none, and bonded with none. Maria continued to feel a void in her personal life, and still often thought about her one true love, Wilhelm. Although whenever she felt the blues coming on, there was enough to keep her busy in her career. Scripts were pouring in by the droves, and she would read each and every one. She was also totally out of touch with the reality of the rest of the world. The country was in the midst of a deep, dark depression. Families who were once prosperous were now literally starving. Little children had no homes to call their own. And fathers and mothers would take any job at all to buy a bit of food or shelter for their families. But the movie industry was thriving because these very same souls needed a break and an escape from their lives. And Maria was just the answer. Soon, everywhere you turned, women all over the country were mimicking her wild hair and sexual look. Maria saw the bread lines and the families sitting in the dirty, damp street gutters, and looked upon them with disdain. Once, she found a tramp digging through the garbage outside her cottage on the hotel grounds, and after calling security, she chased the bony man with a butcher's knife until he ran off the premises.

Patterns Collide 9

The sweat poured down Wilhelm's face as he shoveled his last load of dirt for the day. Ray VanHouten, a local and very successful farmer, had given him a job as a worker. Wilhelm had to swallow a great deal of pride in accepting the job, but he and Henrietta were nearly bankrupt. While Henrietta was making a good salary, they had to pay off debts owed by Wilhelm's business and payments were running behind on their mortgage. At that point he was so desperate, he would have accepted anything.

Wilhelm had just written to his father for the fourth time with no response and he was beginning to think his worst fears had come true, that his father had been put to death for his treason. It was not a happy time, but he was able to keep focused, knowing that every penny he made now was badly needed, and that he was fortunate to have a job at all. Henrietta, on the other hand, had a soaring career as a designer, and had just finished a dress for Vivien Leigh to wear to a charity social.

Word had begun to spread amongst the Hollywood community that she was the designer of choice. All in all, between the two incomes, they were able to keep it together. And during this time, they all grew closer than ever as a family.

One morning Henrietta was sitting in her office, and her secretary buzzed her on the intercom. "Can I come in?" she screeched with an excited twang. "Yes Lucy, what is it?" Henrietta beckoned. "Look at this. It's a letter from Mr. Semple of MGM studios! Maria Cardone has been nominated for the Oscar and he wants you to design her gown! That's amazing! It's just the break you've been waiting for!"

"I won't do it," Henrietta blurted with anger.

Shocked, Lucy asked, "Why not!?"

"That's none of your business. Tell him with all due respect, I refuse," demanded Henrietta.

Puzzled, Lucy typed up the letter. Several days later, she buzzed Henrietta again, and with a tense voice announced, "Mr. Holtman and another gentleman are here to see you."

"Send them in," Henrietta replied.

Henrietta quickly licked her fingers and ran them through her hair to neaten up the few stray strands that were coming out of her bun. She scurried to clean up her desk which was loosely covered with random dress designs she was sketching. As Mr. Holtman entered, he noted how cosmopolitan Henrietta and her office always looked. She had the latest in office technology, fresh trendy colors painted on her walls, and modern office furniture with a door that had a design upholstered on it in a white, leather-like material. A small pink light shined on her desk and it seemed to illuminate her pure white skin. She was dressed neatly and conservatively in a light purple business suit. Mr. Holtman, on the other hand, wore very expensive clothes, but they never looked that way. They were always pushed and tugged by his oversized buttocks and stomach, and his tie never matched his shirt or his jacket. The second man was "very dapper," Henrietta thought to herself. A dark-complexioned man in his late forties or so, his hair was slicked back, and "he looked as if he had come directly from a speakeasy," Henrietta thought.

"This is Mr. Stubin, Henrietta," Mr. Holtman announced. "Mr. Stubin works directly for Mr. Semple of MGM," he continued.

Henrietta began to shrink down in her chair. Mr. Holtman continued, "Mr. Stubin has asked this company to design a gown for Maria Cardone for the Oscars. Naturally, this is a great honor, and you personally should feel even more honored because they have select-ed you, specifically you, to design the gown. Naturally, you will do so with the greatest enthusiasm. Right?" Mr. Holtman said in a threatening manner.

"Naturally, sir," Henrietta gulped.

The two gentlemen exited Henrietta's office and shut the door. Moments later, Lucy was startled by a crash in Henrietta's office. Knowing of her infamous temper, she didn't dare to go in, and could only imagine that the cute little pink lamp that everybody always liked so much was now smashed to pieces on Henrietta's floor.

Henrietta paced her floor rapidly to blow off some steam. She buzzed Lucy to bring in a broom and dustpan, and "Sure enough," thought Lucy, "there's that cute little lamp, and now I have to clean it up." Henrietta lit up a cigarette and then instantly snuffed it out in her ashtray. She turned without a word and slammed the door behind her. "What's got her goat?" she said to herself in disgust. "She gets a chance to design a dress for the hottest star in Hollywood, and she's got a beef with that?"

That night Henrietta sat very quietly at dinner. "You seem very pensive tonight," Wilhelm commented. "You seem quiet Mom," Robert added. "Yeah, what's cooking, Mom?" asked Bill.

Henrietta thought about telling all of them, and then decided it would be too complicated. The fact was that she had to design the gown. Or she would lose her job and then they would be out on the street. She responded that she was tired and retreated to bed.

The next morning she went to work resigned to the fact that she not only had to design a gown for this woman she despised, but it also had to be one of her best. The whole world, especially Mr. Holtman, would be watching with great anticipation. She decided to concentrate on the beauty of the gown only, and put all thought of its recipient out of her mind. Days turned into weeks, but finally she felt she had the perfect design. She personally delivered it to Mr. Holtman. Upon viewing her design, he dashed up from his big leather chair, and gave Henrietta a kiss on the cheek. "It's perfection," he declared. "Why so glum?" he asked.

"No reason, sir." Henrietta left without another word. She decided she needed a breath of fresh air and went for a walk. "Calm down," she said to herself. "Enjoy this. Maria

Cardone doesn't even remember me or my husband. She's a big movie star. And now she's going to make me famous. This is actually my big break. And I know I just designed one of the greatest gowns ever to hit the fashion industry." Henrietta's pace started to pick up as she convinced herself that this was all for the best. "Get over this jealousy. That was all many years ago," she repeated to herself.

Henrietta had first discovered Maria's stardom when she picked up a copy of Photoplay. From that point on, she hid or destroyed any newspaper or magazine that displayed her on the cover so that Wilhelm wouldn't read about her. She didn't know exactly why, but she still felt very threatened by Maria, and was extremely jealous of her success. The last thing she wanted was for Wilhelm to discover her again. However, one day Wilhelm did find Maria's picture on the cover of The New York Times, and to Henrietta's surprise, he shrugged his shoulders and commented, "How far have our morals fallen that a girl like this is an icon?" Henrietta was relieved, and from that point on whenever she ran across an article, she emphasized Wilhelm's comment. He agreed with her.

However, underneath it all, Wilhelm was feeling a burning desire to talk to Maria. He just wanted to find out what happened. After all these years, he had a passionate desire to know if she was involved with taking his money and he also wanted to know more about her pregnancy. And did she ever really love him? He wished she had just disappeared, because now at every newsstand he saw her picture and was reminded of the intense love he once had for her, which brought sadness now. Henrietta, on the other hand, felt nothing but disdain and threatened that she would call the media to alert them to Maria's charade. "This is a tramp of a woman who had a child out of wedlock and gave it up for adoption. Wouldn't the press be interested in learning that?" she often thought with a jealous temper.

As she headed back to her office, she was confronted by a little girl dressed in rags. She was emaciated and dirty. "Could you please spare any money?" pleaded the girl as she looked up at Henrietta with big bright green eyes.

"Where do you live?" Henrietta asked in a soothing tone.

"Right there, ma'am," the little girl whispered, pointing to a woman lying in a cardboard box.

Henrietta gasped as she looked over at the woman who was frail, dirty and just skin and bones. She had bugs crawling in her hair, and a rat scurried out from underneath her torn old wool coat. She looked up at Henrietta, but her eyes were glazed over as if she didn't know where she was. The entire incident hit Henrietta hard. Here she was worrying about petty little jealousies, especially when she had just been given the opportunity of a lifetime. Yet the rest of the world was suffering badly from this depression. These were good people. People who used to have homes and cars and nice clothes, and now they are living in the streets, just barely alive. She felt as though she was living in a beautiful, colorful world, and the rest of the world was still in morbid black and white. Sure they had their problems, but it was nothing like this. The little girl broke her thought pattern when she looked directly into Henrietta's eyes and smiled. "What a sweet smile you have," Henrietta whispered. "I'll bet you would be a beautiful little girl all cleaned up in a nice dress." The little girl's smile broadened and her eyes began to sparkle with life.

"Is that your mommy over there?" Henrietta calmly asked.

"Yes," replied the girl. "But she doesn't talk anymore. I don't think she knows who I am," the girl said shyly with tears welling up in her eyes.

"What's your name sweetheart?"

"Sarah," she responded.

"What a pretty name. Would you like me to talk to your mommy?"

"Oh, would you please help us?" she perked up.

Henrietta went over to talk to her mother, but soon realized that she was very close to death. As she uncovered part of her coat, she could see that some of her skin was rotting away, and all color was gone from her face. Bugs crawled all over her. She had just two teeth left, and she moaned whenever she was touched or spoken to. Henrietta held the little girl's hand and summoned a police officer.

The little girl watched as Henrietta took the officer over to the woman. He took her pulse and they continued in deep discussion, looking over at the little girl every so often.

Henrietta went back over to Sarah and grabbed her hand. She kneeled down and said, "How would you like to come home with me and we'll buy you a new dress and give you a nice hot meal?"

"But what about my mother?" Sarah asked with a worried, puzzled look.

"The police officer is going to get your mother the medical help that she needs. And when she's all better, he knows how to reach me. Is that okay?" she questioned.

Sarah began to cry and looked back at her mother, but when her mother stared into space and didn't seem to recognize her, she looked up at Henrietta and nodded her head.

A new enthusiasm sparked through Henrietta's veins. She immediately took Sarah home and introduced her to the family. Wilhelm was hesitant at first and thought

Henrietta was crazy to get involved. "We have money problems of our own," he scolded. But then he looked over at Sarah and her eyes met his, Henrietta knew the battle was won.

Henrietta took Sarah upstairs and about an hour later they emerged. The boys and Wilhelm were in the parlor, and down the steps came the most beautiful girl they had ever seen. In a dress, with her hair brushed and cleaned, she looked very, very different. To their amazement, they discovered that she wasn't such a little girl after all, but was in all likelihood, even older than Bill!

The boys sat up in their chairs as if a drill sergeant had just entered the room. Robert ran out into the powder room to comb his hair. Then they all went into the dining room for dinner. Sarah ate like she had never seen food before. Robert commented later to Wilhelm that she looked like a wolf. And within days, Wilhelm fell in love with her. She was the daughter they never had. Although they were strangers, she seemed familiar to him, as if she were meant to be part of the family, and he was strangely comfortable with her.

About a week went by, and then one day while the family was sitting in the parlor listening to Wilhelm play the violin, there was a knock at the door. Everyone sat silently for a moment, as there wasn't anyone in the room who didn't anticipate that the day would come. It was the police. Wilhelm and Henrietta met with them out on the front porch and then came back with very somber expressions on their faces. Henrietta took Sarah up to her room to deliver the news. Her mother had died.

Weeks passed and it seemed as though Sarah had become one of the family. She had started to attend school and had already made many friends. The boys noted to Wilhelm that "most of the boys in the school want to get to know her. They all say that she looks like Maria Cardone," Robert quipped.

Wilhelm choked on his pipe. "No, it couldn't be," he thought to himself. "Don't ever mention that to your mother," Wilhelm told Robert. "And tell Bill not to ever mention it either," he warned.

"Why Dad?" he asked.

"Just listen to me, for all of our good," insisted Wilhelm.

The next day was hectic for Henrietta at work. There was a bustle about the office that was unusual from the moment she arrived. "What's going on today?" asked Henrietta. "Tonight is the big night!" Lucy replied with glee. "The Academy Awards! Are you pretending you don't remember? You must be thrilled. Just imagine... Maria Cardone in your dress. It's so exciting. Everyone's buzzing about it, and I hear business is going like gangbusters!"

Falling Apart at the Seams 10

There were lights everywhere as Maria's driver pulled up to the auditorium. Fans lined the streets, screaming and trying to climb over the blockades to get to Maria in her car. "I'm petrified!" Maria confessed. The driver tried to soothe her nerves and offered her a drink of Scotch, which Maria gratefully accepted. "I'm nervous because I'm going to create a big stir tonight if I win," she bragged with an evil grin.

"What do you mean by that?" he asked.

"Oh, you'll see," she replied giggling.

Maria's day had started quite early that morning. She got up and went for a swim in the pool to quiet her tension. And she found that keeping unusual hours was the best way to avoid the throngs of people who would continuously pester her for an autograph.

After a breakfast complete with champagne, she lied around most of the day in her bungalow, wrapped in her robe with nothing else on underneath. Barry Anderson showed up unexpectedly around noon. He was carrying the dress she was to wear. When he arrived, Maria took no notice of him, and instead shrieked with delight at the sight of the green and pearl studded dress. "This is the most beautiful dress I've ever seen!" she screamed as she took it out of his hands. Maria immediately dropped her robe and Barry's quick hands groped her while he had the chance.

"See you tonight," she quipped, pushing him out the door as his hands made their way down her soft white skin. She pushed him out the door and slammed it shut, locking it behind her.

"Come on, let me in!" he yelled.

"No!" Maria bellowed through the door as she

looked the dress over again, getting ready to put it on. "Who's the designer?" Maria yelled.

"Who's the what?"

"Who's the designer? Who designed the dress?" she repeated.

"A Henrietta King from New York. I think that was the name."

"What?! It can't be!" she shrieked. Maria ran over to the phone. "This is Maria Cardone. Get me Shelly Stubin immediately." After a moment, Maria calmly but firmly said "Shelly, I want to know the name of the woman who designed my gown for tonight. Is this the Henrietta King from New York who is married to Wilhelm King?"

Shelly replied, "I don't know who the woman's married to Maria, I just know she's an up-and-coming designer who's handling all of the greats. What's wrong with you? Don't you like the dress?"

"Just get me that information Shelly, and get it now, or I'm not going tonight."

"Maria, are you crazy? You're going to win tonight!" he screamed.

"Get me the information Shelly," she demanded.

"Okay, okay."

Maria went outside nude and dove into the pool to the collective horror and enjoyment of the onlooking sunbathers. She swam lap upon lap to get rid of her anger. Finally, her emotions spent, she went back inside and the phone was ringing. "What?" she asked rudely.

"Maria, yes it's the wife of Wilhelm," Shelly said, puzzled as to why she needed to know this.

Maria slammed the phone down and hurled it across the room.

She stood motionless. "This can't be happening," she thought to herself. "Not on the most important night of my life. I can't make Henrietta famous. She took away Wilhelm, the only thing in my life besides my baby girl that was ever important to me! She's not going to share in my fame!"

Maria frantically looked through her closet for something else to wear.

Suddenly the phone rang again. It was Shelly. "Listen, I told Mr. Semple about your bizarre behavior Maria, and he says you're going and you're going in that dress, or you're gone," he said in a stern voice.

Maria slammed the phone down. Then she got an idea. She would wear the dress and look her best. "I'll fix them," she smirked.

Later, as the chauffeur pulled up in front of the red carpet, Maria leaned forward and kissed him passionately on the lips. The mob went wild. "Ladies and gentlemen... Maria Cardone!" an announcer yelled with excitement.

Maria exited the car by sliding her long bare legs slowly out of the door. Her dress rode up to her underpants as she got out of the car. Again, the crowd cheered with delight.

Maria made her way to her seat, and waited for her category with nervous anticipation. Finally, as if in a dream, her name was called. Tears filled her eyes as she made her way onto the stage. The audience rose to their feet. Maria felt as if it were all happening on a cloud. In slow motion. In a dream. Then she regained her composure.

After making her way through her acceptance speech, she ended it by thanking the woman who designed "this beautiful dress, Mrs. Henrietta King from New York." As the words left her lips she was maneuvering a pocket knife up the side seam of the gown, although this all was hidden by the podium. And as she left the podium, the dress split open and fell to the floor, leaving Maria in only her panties. She at first looked horrified, and then smiled and posed for the photographers, who were frantic with excitement. The crowd was aghast. There were screams, shrieks and pandemonium. Backstage, wrapped in a bathrobe, she played with reporters by flashing them and telling them all with humor, that "it seemed like a good quality dress, but it just fell apart, just like that!"

The next morning's papers carried headlines like "Maria bears her soul," and "Henrietta King, dress designer or burlesque costumer?"

Henrietta was unaware until she made her way to her office through a flurry of reporters and co-workers who were shouting off-color comments. When she entered her office, Mr. Holtman was waiting for her with a box of her belongings. "I don't know what to say Henrietta, except that you've made us a laughing stock."

"But Mr. Holtman, that dress could not have come apart. I supervised the sewing myself," she tried to tell him.

"Henrietta, you're fired," he said firmly and abruptly, while handing her the box.

Henrietta took the box, turned and walked out the door into an outside office that was now filled only with Henrietta's quiet sobbing.

When she returned home, Wilhelm was sitting on the front porch waiting for her. Henrietta somberly approached the screen door, and looked up at Wilhelm's face with a tear falling down her cheek. Suddenly Wilhelm sprang up from the chair and shouted "Welcome home!" As he stood, his pants fell down to his ankles. Henrietta gawked in disbelief, frozen at the entrance of the doorway. From inside the kitchen, out popped Bill, Robert and Sarah.

"Welcome home Mom!" they all yelled gleefully, and at the same time they all dropped their pants. Henrietta stood stunned for a moment and then began to laugh harder and harder, as did the entire family. Instantly, they were able to remove her pain and despair and replace it with laughter. She threw her arms out to signal a hug, and all four of them came running, still laughing as they huddled together. Wilhelm turned to the kids and asked for some privacy with Henrietta. Henrietta agreed and gently warned them to get inside if they didn't want to catch cold. After the children left, Wilhelm and Henrietta sat down on the swing that hung from the front porch ceiling. He placed his arm firmly around Henrietta's thick gray overcoat and squeezed hard. "We'll make it. We always do," he assured her. "I've been thinking about playing the violin professionally."

"You should. You should!" Henrietta said with confidence, looking up into Wilhelm's piercing blue eyes.

"And... I got a cryptic telegram today from Henry Von Stock in Germany. He was a friend of my father's. It said to be patient. And that my father is alive, and will be in touch when he is able to." Wilhelm looked down at Henrietta with a confident smile, trying to hide the extent of his excitement.

Henrietta bounded up out of the swing. "That's great! Aren't you thrilled?"

"Yes, I am. But I don't want to get my hopes up."

"I can understand that." Henrietta said while sitting back down.

The two of them sat for hours with the gentle swing soothing their spirits. A cool breeze had picked up and Wilhelm got up to get a blanket to wrap around them. The wind chimes swayed musically as they watched the sun slowly sink beneath the black outlines of the tree branches overhead. Huddled together that evening, facing almost certain bankruptcy, they felt a calm that they hadn't known before. There was a feeling that everything would be okay, even if it seemed doomed at the moment.

"How could she do something like that?" she asked. "Doesn't she realize that if you and I were revengeful people, we could ruin her? We're probably the only people on the face of the earth who know that she had a child out of wedlock."

"She's an evil person. I'm convinced of that," Wilhelm said somberly.

Then, they sat silently. Wilhelm was thinking about how in love he used to be with Maria. It was the kind of love the public was feeling toward her right now. She was a mystery to him. And even more mysterious was why he had been attracted to her in the first place. Yet, deep down he still felt something toward her, but he couldn't put the feelings in perspective. She was still there though, stirring his soul.

That night, before they went to bed, Henrietta sat at her night table writing a letter. Wilhelm could tell that whatever the letter was, it was personal, and he gave Henrietta the privacy she needed. Henrietta finished the letter and folded it as if to mail it, but instead she stashed it away in the back of her top dresser drawer.

The following weeks were difficult. There were numerous phone calls from bill collectors, and

Henrietta tried her best to feed the family wisely, mainly cooking meals with potatoes to fill them up for as little money as possible. The scariest struggle was with their mortgage. Now four months behind on payment, the bank was sending certified letters threatening to foreclose on the property. Everyone in the family pitched in. Bill, now eleven, had obtained a job at the local drugstore as a soda jerk. Robert went around the neighborhood knocking on doors offering to do any odd jobs that were available, and Sarah helped out by sweeping floors at the beauty parlor. Henrietta took in sewing. Wilhelm kept his job at the farm during the day, and then he worked playing the violin in New York City at night. It was an exhausting schedule, but he found playing his violin to be exhilarating. And each time the bank sent a letter threatening foreclosure, they were collectively able to gather just enough money together to hold it off. On those rare occasions when all of them were home for dinner, they would turn the discussion into a family meeting, deciding who would do what to make money, and how much would be enough. They worked together as a team, and as much as it seemed like hardship, they were actually accomplishing something, and that felt good. It was the closest the family had felt to each other.

Henrietta noticed that Sarah, who had calculated her age to be about twelve, was quickly becoming a beauty. She had thought several times about getting her into the modeling field.

Star Dust *11*

After the last party had nearly ended, Maria accepted a ride from Barry Anderson. Barry was the epitome of a handsome leading man, and Maria was the quintessential leading lady who had had too much champagne. Barry sent his wife home from the party early, explaining that he would suffer through to the end to kiss up to the Hollywood executives that could further his career. Maria was dressed in a large man's shirt, and was eyed by every male in the room for the entire evening.

Maria and Barry said their goodbyes and left in Barry's car. The roof was off and the warm breeze flowed through Maria's long raven colored hair as they drove up the coast.

The sound of the ocean had a soothing effect on Maria, and her shirt began to fly up in the wind, exposing her underpants as they drove. Barry found it very difficult to concentrate on the road. As they approached the Beverly Hills Hotel, Maria leaned over and kissed Barry on the side of his lips. "Green light!" Barry thought to himself. The staff of the hotel had lit the fireplace in the cozy cottage and the sitting room was full of gardenias sent by various admirers. Maria and Barry entered the cottage arm in arm, and Maria almost fell a few times on the way in. She was even more intoxicated than she had originally thought. As she tripped into the sitting area, Barry caught her and spun her around. Grabbing her arms with both hands he pulled her tightly and kissed her. She responded. As they kissed his hands caressed her body, first from outside of her shirt and then from underneath. His narrow, manicured fingers frantically unbuttoned, while trying to make sure Maria paid little attention to what he was doing. Finally, he maneuvered the shirt and gleefully watched it fall to the floor in a white cotton heap. Excitedly, he pressed up against Maria's pure, pristine skin. His nostrils flaring with passion as he savored her flowery scent.

"What are you doing?!" she shrieked.

"You know what I'm doing," he said softly.

"Get out of here!" Maria screamed.

Maria was frantic. As she emerged from her drunken stupor, she didn't like what was happening. Maria had not been intimate with a man since she was raped. And the only man she had ever felt she trusted or loved enough to have those feelings for was married and living in New York!

She screamed, "Stop it! Stop it! Stop it, Robert!"

"Robert? Who the heck is Robert?" Barry asked, angrily.

"Just leave me alone!" Maria yelled, while trying to pull away from him.

The hotel security knocked at the door frantically. "Are you all right Miss Cardone?" they yelled through the door.

"No! Help me!" she screamed.

As security swiftly let themselves in, Barry slapped her across the face and in one violent motion, threw her against the couch, brushing by the astonished security guards as he walked out. Cameras were everywhere, and Maria remembered only seeing flashes of white as she lay still against the couch in only her underpants. She stood up and screamed at the security guards to get out of her room and leave her alone. Then she quickly pushed her body up against the door to block the world out.

She slumped back against the door and slowly lowered herself to the floor where she curled up with her knees to her chest, sobbing. It was at that moment that she realized that she had to find Wilhelm. It was the only way she could go on with her life. It had to be resolved.

The next morning she contacted her agent. "I need to get out of here, to avoid all of the publicity," she pleaded. "I want to go to New York."

"Okay, I'll arrange it. It's probably a good idea. Since this whole episode with your striptease at the Academy Awards and then the attempted rape by Barry Anderson, you're as hot as they come baby!" he said excitedly. "But it would be a good idea for you to lay low for awhile. I would suggest disguising yourself, and I'll send a driver once the train is booked."

Maria began packing, and when she was finished, she stuffed her hair up into a wide brimmed hat, wrapped a scarf around her neck, put on jeans and a sweatshirt, removed all of her makeup, and put on her biggest sunglasses to cover her face. The train was booked and the car arrived, just as she was finishing up. When she arrived in New York she was met by another driver who took her to the Plaza. Her room was reserved under the name of Amy Smith. It was a beautiful room, looking out over Central Park, and she sat for a while watching the horse and buggy carriages drive tourists around the busy streets. It was beginning to snow and the city looked so pretty coated in white. Not at all like she had remembered it.

On Saturday morning she had arranged for a taxi to take her to Montclair to see Wilhelm's house. She still wasn't sure exactly what she would do, but she at least wanted to see where he lived. Once they arrived in Montclair, she asked the taxi driver to park inconspicuously down the road a bit from the house so that she could sit and watch the comings and goings. To her surprise, it was a nice home. She had expected something much less! And they were having a yard sale. It looked like they were selling some very beautiful furnishings.

In fact, they were selling some of their most beautiful furnishings. It was Henrietta's idea. A desperate attempt to save their home. But few people attended the sale, because few people had any money at all.

At last, Maria spotted Wilhelm. She held her breath as he walked out onto the lawn, carrying a large overstuffed chair that had been in Henrietta's family for generations. He looked almost exactly the same as he did on the ship, only, he had aged some. But he looked even more handsome. Distinguished. "I'm still in love with him," Maria thought to herself, clutching her heart. "And they must be poor. They must be desperate if they're selling such beautiful heirlooms," she thought while smiling over their anguish.

"Ma'am this is going to cost you a fortune," the taxi driver reminded her as they sat waiting with the meter running.

She scoffed at his reminder.

In fact, Maria was right. The Kings were desperate. As they were all pitching in to move the furniture one by one, Maria saw Wilhelm's children. When Sarah emerged from the house, she was wiping off some old crystal goblets that Henrietta kept in the dining room's built-in cabinets. Henrietta, who was standing on the lawn arranging furniture, noticed a necklace on Sarah that she hadn't seen before. "What's this?" she asked smiling, as she took the necklace in her hand.

It was nothing much. Just a silver ring on a simple cord.

"Oh, I've been keeping this in my pocket. But I found this cord in the house. I hope you don't mind," she replied shyly.

"Not at all," quipped Henrietta. "I just had

never seen this before. Where did you get it?"

"It was my mother's," she replied looking up into Henrietta's eyes while squinting to avoid the sunlight. "My birth mother's. Not my adoptive mother's," she said.

Henrietta's knees buckled and she abruptly sat back onto a chair that had been placed behind her. "You mean that the woman who I found you with was your adoptive mother?" she asked, in shock.

"Yes," Sarah answered, looking down at the ground. "And this is the one possession that my birth mother had," she continued.

"You poor baby," Henrietta rose and hugged Sarah.

"It's okay, I'm happier here with you and this family then I've ever been in my life. It's like a dream come true for me."

Henrietta held her tightly for a while and then backed away a bit. "Let me see this," she said smiling. Henrietta ran her fingers over the ring. "Oh, it looks like real silver," she said, trying to make Sarah feel the ring was of value. Then she flipped the ring over to see the sterling marking. Next to the mark was an inscription. "Did you know there's an inscription in here?" Henrietta announced.

"No, I didn't have any idea..." she replied. "What does it say?"

Henrietta squinted and turned the ring in different directions. She read the inscription to herself. "To Wilhelm, love Mom."

Henrietta fell back into the chair.

"Are you okay? You're as white as a sheet," Sarah observed, puzzled by Henrietta's sudden behavior.

"Sit down child," Henrietta pleaded.

"I'm very superstitious with this type of thing. I believe firmly that such a family heirloom must be carried close to your heart. You must never wear this outside of your clothing. Do you understand? It's very important to me," she said sternly, gasping for air as she spoke while stuffing the necklace into Sarah's shirt.

Sarah was puzzled but she agreed. She didn't

see any harm in adhering to Henrietta's non-sensical request.

"Okay now, run along, we have plenty of work to do," she commanded.

Henrietta sat motionless, staring but not seeing anything. "What does this all mean?" she repeated over and over to herself.

In the distance she spotted an old, handsome looking man walking slowly down the sidewalk toward their house. As she looked in the other direction, she spotted a woman emerging from a taxicab. She held her breath as the woman got closer. "It's Maria Cardone. I would know her anywhere," she thought to herself. She stared at Maria as she approached, but Maria stopped a few houses down the road and stood to observe the family. She was wearing a black scarf encircling her face with large sunglasses, but there was no question in Henrietta's mind. It was surely Maria.

The rest of the family was still busy at work. There were some potential customers milling about. Again Henrietta's eyes fixated on Maria.

Suddenly she heard Wilhelm scream. It was a startling sound that she had never heard before. Wilhelm stood in the corner of the yard hugging the old man. Henrietta and the children ran over to them. Wilhelm, with tears rolling down his face exclaimed, "This is my dad!"

Wilhelm was wrought with so much emotion that he could hardly speak. This was a dream of his, but one that he thought would never come true. He loved his father more than anything, and it was a piece of his life that had been missing for too long a time.

Wilhelm introduced Henrietta and the children one by one, and the old man passionately hugged and kissed them all. Wilhelm grabbed onto Henrietta and kissed her. Henrietta looked down the street. Maria had started to approach, but then stopped again, and repeated this motion several times.

As the family moved into the house, Wilhelm's father asked him why they were selling such beautiful furniture. Wilhelm explained his initial success and what the Great Depression had done to his wealth. His father handed him an envelope. Wilhelm took the pouch from his father's frail, shaking hand.

"For you son," his father said gently.

Wilhelm opened the envelope which was full of cash. He looked up at his father in astonishment, trying to focus through the tears that filled his eyes. The boys let out a cheer and ran outside. They started pulling their belongings out of the shoppers' hands, and as quickly as possible they pulled their possessions back inside the house.

"But how dad?" Wilhelm asked, still astonished.

"When the war approached and you went off to America, Mom and I buried this money in the forest. It was always meant for you. It's yours," he said, stroking Wilhelm's hair.

Wilhelm sank to his knees and cried.

Sarah and the boys hugged him.

Picking Wilhelm's chin up with his hand so that he would look into his eyes, his dad said quietly, "You've had wealth all along Wilhelm.

And I'm not referring to the money I just gave you, or to the money you've earned throughout your life. You've had riches that far exceed the dreams of princes and kings."

Wilhelm appeared puzzled.

"Your wealth is right here in this room. It's the love of your family. It's something that money can't buy."

Henrietta clenched her teeth to hold back the tears. And then she remembered Maria. She ran upstairs and grabbed the letter she had stashed in the back of her drawer. She stuffed it into an envelope, addressed it, and ran outside. The postman was just passing by and she called out to him. Maria still stood frozen in place on the sidewalk. Henrietta stared at her as she handed the postman the letter. Maria realized that Henrietta recognized her and turned to walk away.

The postman read the envelope, "Wow, you're writing to Louella Parsons? She's the most powerful gossip columnist in Hollywood. They say she can make or break a career," he said as he walked away, stuffing the letter into his bag.

Coming soon,
from Ken Koenig!

Legal Rape.

The legal drama of a small

business owner caught in

the web of the dysfunctional

judicial system, and a case

that should have never been.

This one will have you reeling

in disgust and disbelief, and

doubting the fortitude of your

constitutional rights!